MURDER
IN AN OHIO
RIVER TOWN

Book Design & Production:
Columbus Publishing Lab
www.ColumbusPublishingLab.com

Copyright © 2024 by
Janet Shailer

All rights reserved.
This book, or parts thereof,
may not be reproduced
in any form without permission.

Paperback ISBN: 978-1-63337-833-9
E-Book ISBN: 978-1-63337-834-6

Printed in the United States of America
1 3 5 7 9 10 8 6 4 2

MURDER
IN AN OHIO
RIVER TOWN

A NOVEL BY
JANET SHAILER

proving press

CHAPTER 1

Hot summer days in Steubenville always have a lingering odor to them. One hundred years ago, the steel mills and chemical plants in the area would emit a wave of pungent smells that seeped into every pore of one's body. It was as if the collective sweat of the working class mixed with rotten eggs and permeated everything. Parts of it remain.

Steubenville sits beside the Ohio River and has a long history of being a blue-collar town. Beer brewing began here in 1815 and was a major industry for many years. Seventy-five years later the steel mills in Steubenville and nearby Weirton, West Virginia, added to the saloons' coffers when men rushed out of work to seek a glass of beer alongside John Barleycorn and wash the soot out of their mouths.

Today is one of those days my grandmother would call "close"—close to 100 degrees Fahrenheit and 100% humidity. I'm not in the mood to visit with my elderly mother but, as her only child, I feel an obligation. I pull my car into the parking lot of Silver Belles Long-Term Care Center and go inside. The sweat is glistening on my neck as I plop into a broken chair next to Gracie's bed. Slivers of June sun dart through cracks in the horizontal window blinds. I can tell Gracie is in a sour mood.

"I'm cold," my 82-year-old mother says bluntly.

"It's 93 degrees outside," I say.

"I need another blanket," she demands.

The 10 x 12 hospital-type room that enfolds Gracie is a poorly accessorized cell. A third grader's handmade Valentine is taped to the wall—a missive sent from the great-grandson she no longer recognizes.

"Is it snowing outside?" Gracie asks.

"No, it's sweltering."

"I need gloves."

A short glance around the room is a repetitious movie loop that has not changed in one full year. A forlorn Christmas tree sits on a corner table with a spider crawling along a dusty limb. A calendar is push-pinned on the wall near Gracie's pillow. A half-eaten cookie sits on her bedside table. A stack of adult diapers sits in a corner with soiled Ace bandages draped over them.

Gracie is a mental and physical wreck stuck inside a skeletal frame. But she is my mother and I need to pry some things out of her. My grandchildren's futures may depend on whether I can glean important family history from her before she dies.

"Your grandmother was here this morning," she says.

"That's interesting, Mom, since she's been dead for 23 years."

"She's not dead. She comes in and talks to me. I told her I won the lottery. She said you need to take the money to the bank. Make sure to get a receipt."

I sigh and step off the ride on the Crazy Train Express. Last week my mother was stewing about not having any money. This week she thinks she is a millionaire.

I stop at the nurse's station and ask a few questions. I've gotten to know the staff well in the year she has been here at Silver Belles.

"You know, Maureen, your mother could live for months like this or years," the head nurse says. "We should have more lab results tomorrow."

The endless string of lab tests never reveals the full picture. Same scenario every time. Nobody knows.

I stop by Gracie's room to tell her I'll return later.

"Did you find your key?"

"I don't need a key, Mom. I just walk inside."

"You can't get the baubles if you don't have the key."

I am too busy to listen to more nonsense so I drive out to Gracie's storage unit to continue the process of sorting her belongings. Gracie is never going to live alone again. I have her power of attorney so the dreaded process of maintaining her belongings and paying her bills is my responsibility.

Most of her furniture and clothes have been given away. A wooden chest, three filing cabinets, several photo albums, and a painting of her favorite childhood pet—a dachshund named Fritz—are among the things stored there. Her jewelry box has been stored in the closet at my home but I have opened it only once in the last year. I rarely wear jewelry and I always felt those things are too personal to the owner.

Gracie never talks about her jewelry. What propelled her to mention gems to me today? Delusions are not uncommon after a stroke. Neither are fantasies. I dismiss it.

There is one item in the corner of the storage unit that I have never touched. It is a shoe box wrapped tightly with old electrical wire, of all things. Gracie once told me never to open it, and I laugh out loud remembering how I once thought anything MacGyvered together like that probably contains explosives. It's time to know its contents.

I plop the box in my car and drive home. I ply the wires off and sigh, realizing Gracie will never know I've disobeyed her orders. I lift the lid and a musty smell emanates. On top is an old magazine article with a photo of a grave, a postcard from Green Mountain National Park, a matchbook from a place called the Holiday House, rosary beads, and a man's garnet ring. The ring is unusual. It has two tiny diamonds on either side of the garnet—almost like a wedding ring.

Upon further inspection inside the box, I find an old driver's license with the name Carlton Bergstrom, a cousin of my father. He is the same man who is rumored to be the person who allegedly poisoned my father years ago. The items must have belonged to either my father or his cousin. Very strange. I must find out.

I pour myself some Riesling and wait before I explore any other contents. My mother never talks about my father. Any inquiries are quickly rebuffed. She raised me from age six in a modest home just south of Steubenville, Ohio, in a village called Mingo Junction. Originally known as Mingo Bottom or Mingo Town, it was the starting point for the ill-fated Crawford expedition against Native Americans in 1782. By the early 1900s, Carnegie Steel (later Wheeling-Pittsburgh Steel) had erected a plant in Mingo. Grandpa Gino's father and uncle, both Italian immigrants, worked there.

Gracie worked as a nurse to support the two of us. On Saturdays she would supplement her income by doing respite care for elderly patients in their homes. She would always have me tag along on those days. Sundays, however, were our special times to spend together. Occasionally we'd drive to Wheeling to do something fun—if her budget allowed.

My father, Jefferson Bergstrom, Jr., is a total enigma to me. Maybe now I can find out something about his life and a clue to his death. His case was never solved by the Steubenville Police Department. Is it possible that at age 62 I can finally solve the puzzle?

I grab my magnifying glass and look closely at the newspaper clipping. The article and grave marker photo turn out to be a story about Chief Cornplanter in the Cornplanter Cemetery, Warren County, Pennsylvania. I search my iPad sources for the history of this Seneca war chief. I find he fought in both the French & Indian War and the American Revolution on the British side.

I find this fascinating. Even though I am a retired history teacher, I know little about the Seneca and other Native Americans who inhabited Mingo Junction in the late 1700s. Ohio history sources call my hometown the 'Gateway into Ohio Country' because pioneers traveled the Ohio River from Ft. Pitt and often stopped here and headed west by foot or ox cart. In my years of teaching, I only mentioned to my students a dab about Mingo Junction and its historic significance to Native Americans and the white settlers who came as the Northwest Territories opened in 1787.

I pick up the postcard of Green Mountain National Park. I see that it is in Vermont near the New York border. Did Gracie once visit there? I look closer at the ring. There are no markings inside the band. Whose is it? Could the park, Chief Cornplanter, and the ring be more clues in unraveling the mystery surrounding my father? Now this is a mystery worthy of a novel.

I pull into Silver Belles Long-term Care Center and find my mother sitting in a Broda chair in the dining room. "I took the bus to Beaver Falls last night so I could go dancing," Gracie says. "Frank Sinatra showed up and sang for us."

"That's nice, Mom," I say, knowing she only dreamed it. For starters, Gracie cannot walk, let alone dance. "What did Frank sing?"

"All his hits. Some of us got up and jitterbugged."

I find it interesting that Gracie mentions Beaver Falls. I know our family doesn't have any connection to western Pennsylvania. I try to get her to tell me more about it.

"There's a roadhouse outside town with really good food. Your grandmother got mad when she found out I went."

I attempt to pump her for more info but she was more interested in folding her napkin than talking anymore. The only thing I know about Beaver Falls is that it is an hour's drive away and the home of Joe Namath, the NFL Hall of Fame quarterback.

Kayla Banks, the facility's social worker, spies me and asks if I have a minute to talk. I leave Gracie still engrossed in her napkin and walk to a nearby office.

"Gracie has been a little upset lately," Kayla says. "She insists her husband keeps coming in to see her."

"That can't be. Gracie never talks about my father. I only know his name."

"Is it Carlton?"

I'm dumbfounded. I explain that Carlton was my father's cousin and that my father, Jefferson Bergstrom, died right before my birth 62 years ago. Gracie dropped Bergstrom and returned to her maiden name. She changed my last name too. I grew up as Maureen Rivers, not Bergstrom.

"Interesting," Kayla says. "I'll tell the staff."

I leave Silver Belles and drive immediately to the Steubenville library. I ask the information associate how to access their genealogy technology on one of their in-house computers. Within 15 minutes I'm diving into a list of people with the last name Bergstrom. I feel like I'm intruding on strangers' lives yet I'm determined to find a link to my past.

I find a bit of a thread with a few Bergstrom surnames. An hour later I get the idea to enlist the help of a professional genealogist. The library's information associate has the name of one. I scribble down the contact information and make a beeline home to my desktop computer. I've always found that I work better on major projects at my desktop. All my lesson plans for teaching, all my banking, and all my medical information are stored there. My late husband, Anders Albrecht, always insisted we use a separate email address on the desktop than the ones we use on our iPad tablets.

I feel relaxed and in charge when I'm sitting at my desk. I've even written several historical articles for the *Herald-Star*, Steubenville's daily newspaper. People say I have a knack for writing. Many of those articles have to do with Steubenville's reputation as a river gambling town. It's also the birthplace of singer Dean Martin. Mingo Junction is just a quick drive from there.

I send an inquiry to the professional genealogist and try to relax. I give her the few names and dates I've collected and the fact I only have my father's name and no other information about him. I cross my fingers that her fee will not be cost-prohibitive. I just retired from 37 years of teaching so I live comfortably but not extravagantly. I've always been frugal, just like my mother.

 I fall asleep with the satisfaction that if I find nothing, it's not the end of the world. I've lived 62 years not knowing anything about the Bergstroms. But their ghosts are haunting me.

CHAPTER 2

I wake up startled at 4 a.m. drenched in sweat. I've just had a vivid nightmare where I dreamed my Grandpa Gino, who everyone called Big G, was involved in a shooting at an illegal gambling house (not his).

"NO, STOP!" I shout into the darkness before becoming fully conscious. It startles my dog Silky, who cocks her head and jumps off the bed in a huff.

In my dream my Grandma Viviana was frantically calling the police, but they refused to come because the joint was unlawful, tainted, and a den of iniquity.

I was very close to both my maternal grandparents when I was younger. Until I was age 6, Gracie and I lived with them. My Grandpa Gino owned Big G's Cigars—one of several gambling dens in town. It doubled in its early Prohibition days as a speakeasy. During Gino's teenager years, he ran numbers for the owner of the establishment. Later, as his personal wealth grew, he bought the building. Several types of gambling occurred at Big G's. There were card and dice games 24/7 and bets on horse racing in the afternoon. If there was a vice to be found, you could find it somewhere in Steubenville.

Conveniently my grandmother owned a stationery store called Passages around the corner. As a nod to the kids in the community, she kept a comic book rack near the cash register and sold them for a dime. She had several favorite kids who would stop at the store, and she gave them penny candy. As an additional service to the community, she sold the daily newspaper that contained the three-digit numbers used to run the "handle" in the numbers racket.

As the business enterprise flourished, Gino bought a car wash on the outskirts of town—presumably to launder his money. During my own teenage years, grandpa sent me there to retrieve coins in the collection box.

While growing up, Big G was my substitute father. He was a jovial fellow most of the time and was generous to my mother and grandmother. However, I often heard whispered rumors that Big G ran a tight ship at the cigar store and could knock a man down with a wicked right hook if provoked. There was even a rumor that Big G once killed a man and deposited the body in the deepest part of the Ohio River. By 1960, the year of my birth, most of the corruption had been cleaned up. But not all.

History shows that by 1890 Ohio had become the second largest producer of steel in the nation. That combination really made Steubenville click. Shipping along the river was heavy. Steel and other goods traveling from Pittsburgh to Cincinnati to Chicago floated right by Steubenville. Here began the area's growing dependency on thirsty sailors who frequented some of the town's 80 saloons. Sailors loved to troll Water Street where there were brothels stocked with "soiled doves" (ladies of the evening) to show them a good time. By 1904 there were occasional "saloon boats" swimming in the waters—a form of floating distilleries.

Steubenville was also a kind of river town with many hidden doors. That came in handy in the 1920s when Prohibition gripped America. Soon afterwards the town's then 100 saloons closed, but men and women still pined for refreshments. Now behind those hidden doors were an abundance of speakeasies. Facades abounded with a wink and a nod to the authorities. Pool rooms presented themselves as legitimate business establishments, while trips through hidden passages took you to "parlors" complete with gambling, booze, and loose women.

The southern part of the city was known as the Badlands. Federal dry agents roamed the city—brave fellows with short life expectancies. From 1920-1933, Steubenville had the record for most dry agents murdered. In 1926 alone, there was a spell of 12 murders in three months. South Sixth Street became known as the "death district."

During Prohibition, Ohio's women had a reputation for vigilance against alcohol and public drunkenness. The Women's Christian Temperance Union (WTCU) was founded in Hillsborough (Highland County) in 1873 and later moved to Cleveland. In the late 1850s, Westerville (near Columbus) was one of the first communities to ban alcohol. The Anti-Saloon League later moved its headquarters there. Their hard work helped bring us Prohibition.

Blind Tiger (illegal liquor) was everywhere. It didn't take long for the gangland-style murders to begin. The Black Hand crime organization was accused of at least 29 murders in Jefferson

County. Vice crimes were often overlooked, and Steubenville's good citizens screamed about political corruption. Meanwhile, bribes were thrown around like candy at a Fourth of July parade. The city continued to lose revenue while others made money.

A river gambling town like Steubenville was always a boiling cauldron of rumors. They didn't call it "Little Chicago" for nothing. During my fourth-grade year, two of my classmates disappeared in one week. Rumors swirled that one student's father had turned up dead during a drug bust, and the other had a mother who allegedly stole money from a non-profit organization. I never saw either classmate again.

On the other hand, if the local Catholic church needed to fill bins with Christmas presents for underprivileged kids, Big G promptly took care of it. When my public elementary school had a canned-goods drive for needy families, Big G showed up with a truckload.

My grandparents never broke the two unwritten laws in our family—1) never speak the word "gambling," and 2) never utter the word "Bergstrom" in any way, shape, or form.

I anxiously await a report from my newly hired genealogist with clues to my Bergstrom family history. I would have never done this if Gracie was not incapacitated inside an awful form of medical purgatory. She is not sick enough to die but not well enough to hope to get better. Her legs are like rubber and sometimes her speech is incoherent.

This morning's copy of the *Herald Star* is on the coffee table, seeming to call my name. The paper has been in publication for over 200 years. It's like an old friend. On page 3 is a story revealing that the building that once housed my grandmother's stationery store is being renovated. Interesting items have been found behind some drywall and under a floorboard, including a New York license plate from 1959—the year before my birth.

I try not to get a speeding ticket as I drive to the Steubenville police headquarters. I show a desk officer the article and explain politely that my name is Maureen Albrecht and my grandmother owned the building named in the article during that time. Could I see the items found?

It takes a while to get a response, but finally a uniformed officer ushers me back to an office in the bowels of the building. Another officer asks me to sit. He tells me his last name is Gambino. My active imagination associates his last name with the New York mob of the 1950s and '60s. Ugh.

"So, you are related to Gino and Viviana Rivers?" he asks with all the emotion of a crashtest dummy.

I wasn't expecting him to use my grandparents' names. I swallow hard. "I am their granddaughter."

"Viviana owned the building that once housed Big G's Cigar Store, right?" Gambino snarls.

"Yes," I say, as I remember Gino put everything in Viviana's name in case he got sued or went to jail.

The officer deposits a box in front of me that now somehow appears like an accessory to a crime. How many police shows have I watched where this kind of thing occurs? I should have stayed home.

"Here's some things we found," Gambino barks.

I stare into the box and gasp. There is the New York license plate mentioned in the newspaper, a postcard from Barton Mines in Johnsburg, New York, a gold and diamond bracelet, a bag of

IOUs, and a photo of my mother at her high school graduation. I look up at Gambino and see he has a slight smirk on his face.

"We also found this buried in the wall," he says, holding up a piece of metal with a crack down the middle.

"What is it?"

"It's a currency plate used by the federal government in making dollar bills," he says. "There's always crooks who want to try and print ten-dollar bills. It's highly illegal to have one of these. The FBI will be checking this out."

I swallow again and pray that we are finished. Just then the officer reaches into his desk drawer and, with great flair, pulls out a gun and waves it two feet from my nose. It's a World War II-era Glock pistol once used by the German Luftwaffe.

"This gun has been traced to your grandfather. You can have everything in the box except the Glock and the currency plate," Gambino says. "We're keeping them as possible evidence."

I want to vomit.

• • •

"Gracie," I say gently, tapping my mother's shoulder. "Are you awake?"

"What day is it?" she asks.

"Tuesday, June 14."

"I've been waiting all day to take the bus to heaven."

Gracie doesn't know what day it is let alone where she is or even that she's in Steubenville. It's sad to see her like this so I hit the 'play' button on a CD player I bought for her. The music of Glen Miller soothes her.

"Are we going to the Capitol Ball Room tonight for the big band concert?" she asks.

I cringe. The Capitol Ball Room is where she went to dance as a young woman. It had to be the best time of her life—a time before her brief marriage to Jefferson Bergstrom. A time before the complexities and unfairness of life began.

"No, the Capitol Ball Room is closed for repairs," I lie. It has been closed for years but I don't want to upset Gracie.

"Who is your favorite singer?" I ask.

"Frank Sinatra. He was a river rat just like all the boys in town. Just like Dean." River rat is a term often used for Steubenville's boys since we live next to the Ohio River.

I see an opening to ask a gambling question. It's always been a taboo subject but I go for it.

"Was Frank a gambler?"

"Sure. Everybody knows that."

"Did anyone in Steubenville know him personally?"

A look crosses Gracie's face that I have never seen before. She looks puzzled at first, then smiles with a faraway glaze in her eyes.

"I don't remember."

There used to be a spiderweb of connections between Steubenville and the Las Vegas casino gambling operations. "Little Chicago" had a complete network of gambling personnel from Pittsburg, Youngstown, Cleveland, and Wheeling. Steubenville was a pipeline for blackjack and craps dealers to the Nevada casinos. Furthermore, the Pittsburgh-Youngstown-Steubenville connection practically became the nation's training ground for bookmakers.

I switch subjects and talk about family members—she likes that.

"I saw your Aunt Bee yesterday," Gracie says.

"Really, how interesting." My Aunt Beatrice, known as Bee, has been dead for 15 years.

"Yes, did she ever tell you about that horrible attack on her after Kennedy was shot?"

My Aunt Bee did, in fact, once encounter an angry, senile man as she worked in the Steubenville library. The man was in the throes of a very bad day in late November of 1963. He walked with a cane and had no one with him to assist his journey through the library. The man encountered Bee as she was shelving books in the fiction section.

"May I help you, sir?" Bee had asked.

The man immediately started screaming about Lee Harvey Oswald and Jimmy Hoffa. Before Bee could call for help, the man raised his cane and tried to strike her across the head. Bee took the book she was holding and raised it high enough to block the hit. The man fell over backward and passed out—much to the horror of nearby patrons. The book, ironically, was *War and Peace*.

"That was a terrible thing that happened," I say to Gracie.

"That crazy man was in the mafia," Gracie says adamantly. "He was a friend of Jack Ruby."

Now it is my turn to gasp. What is my mother talking about? Can these lapses between actual memory and fantasy hold a crumb of truth? Or has she dreamed it by watching too many movies over the years? She had indeed loved Jack Kennedy—the nation's first Catholic president. I was only three years old that November, but I remember my mother's tears flowed like the Ohio River after a 4-inch rain as she watched tiny John Kennedy Jr. salute his father's coffin. Gracie still has the *Life* magazine photos from that week.

I can see that Gracie is tiring so I leave and head to the Steubenville library—the same one where Aunt Bee had worked. I walk to the information desk and tell the associate that I need to know about the Barton Mines in upstate New York. Within minutes I have before me two books about mines and a DVD to take home. I walk out wishing Aunt Bee was still here.

I dive into the information and find the mine operated until 1984 and is near Lake George. I remember that Gracie had an ashtray from Lake George when I was a teenager. The mine has minerals called rutile which form needle-like crystals. If they orient along the crystal axes, they may cause asterism—a starlight luminous figure.

I discover the Barton Garnet Mines are some of the world's largest. Ironically, the garnet is both Gracie's and my birthstone. Is this a sign or a wild goose chase? I thumb through information to find that the mines were found by Henry Hudson Barton in 1878. The original mine was located near the summit of Gore Mountain in Adirondack Park. In the early years, raw garnet was transported by train to New York City or Philadelphia for crushing and processing. This fulfilled the demand for garnet abrasives. The garnets are found in outcroppings along stream beds, so Barton bought the whole mountain.

Clues are starting to collect in this wackadoodle search for my Bergstrom relatives. I try to think how my grandfather's illicit business could tie into the Bergstrom mystery. Could the cousins have been people who frequented Big G's? I have never met anyone, except Gracie's best friend, Charisse Duhamel, who ever said he or she knew my father or his cousin.

Several years ago, without Gracie knowing, I went to the Jefferson County Courthouse to search through records to try and find my parents' marriage license. I came up empty. Obviously my parents were married somewhere else. But with these new clues maybe I can find out if they were married in Pennsylvania or even New York. I've decided I should engage my trusted daughter Bridgette in the search.

My iPhone rings—it's Bridgette, and I wonder if she has read my mind. Unfortunately, she has a semi-emergency.

"Mom, Max has an earache so I'm taking him to the doctor. We can't have dinner together tonight. Maybe tomorrow."

Max is my eight-year-old grandson. He has an autoimmune disease that flares up on occasion. The doctors have asked many times for our family medical history to try and get a better handle on his care. Since my father's history is a blank slate, I'm stuck on that trail. Max's twin sister, Olivia, seems to be very healthy.

Now that dinner with my daughter and grandkids is cancelled, I decide to pick up a pizza and gorge myself in front of the TV while streaming *The Shining*. I have a love-hate relationship with horror movies, and I must be in the right mood. I'm in one of those moods now where I want to be entertained by homicidal maniacs.

I pull into Jailhouse Pizza and get in line. The building has various photos and drawings of mobsters—everyone from Alphonse Capone to Bugs Moran. I scan the wall and my eyes are drawn to one photo. It looks for all the world like my grandfather as a young man standing next to some thugs. I gulp.

I hustle back home with my favorite onion and cheese pie and pour myself a generous glass of Merlot. It's at times like these that I miss the companionship of my late husband. I hate being a widow, but I have no other choice. I turn on the TV, grab a blanket, and settle back for a movie thriller. I get to the scary part, and my cell phone rings. I almost jump through the ceiling. The caller ID reveals it is the Steubenville police department. Now that they know I'm a local link to Gino Rivers, I suspect they are digging up dirt.

"Is this Maureen Albrecht?" a male voice says.

"Yes." I brace myself for what is next.

"We'd like to see you again tomorrow."

• • •

I spend another sleepless night trying to figure out why the police want to see me. I feel the need for some moral support, and I, of course, think of my daughter. Bridgette has always been level-headed with a wicked sense of humor. I met her father, Anders Albrecht, in high school, but we never hung out together or dated then. We both, ironically, chose the same college, and during our first semester he offered to give me a ride home for Thanksgiving break. By spring we were dating. He became a biology teacher, but left the profession after a few years to purchase an electronics store. All was going well until Anders reached the age of 56. In 2015, he was diagnosed with cancer and went through all the treatments. Unfortunately, we lost him in 2018. Bridgette was 36 and the twins were four.

I decide I will tell Bridgette about the police visits tonight. I need a sympathetic ear.

"Well, Mrs. Albrecht, I see you've returned," an officer says. "It's good to see my favorite teacher."

I realize he is one of my former students, Timmy Konig, who graduated 15 years ago. That kind of thing happens to me all the time—former students who say how much they loved my class, although I suspect they are fibbing.

"Sergeant Gambino wants me to send you back to his office."

I study the floor as I trudge once again into the bowels of the station. I sit at the same gray metal desk as before, dreading my fate.

"Hello, Mrs. Albrecht," Sergeant Gambino says with a touch of whimsy. "Officer Konig tells me you are a history teacher."

I nod.

"Have you ever studied the history of the Native Americans in eastern Ohio and western Pennsylvania?"

"Somewhat," I say.

"Are you familiar with Native American artifacts."

"I know the difference between an arrowhead and a hatchet. That's about it."

"After finding the currency plate in the wall of your grandmother's old Passages store, I had some of the officers dig through items in our evidence room from suspected crimes committed here in town. Some are traced to your grandfather, Gino Rivers."

"I see."

"Among the items are Native American stem pipes worth a fortune, dozens of arrowheads, and a silver gorget that is practically priceless. We found them under the floorboards at his old cigar store after he died and the building was sold."

I stare at Gambino in total disbelief.

"That's not all. There is a bag of garnets. We have no idea what those are worth."

I'm stumped. I have no knowledge of my grandfather being involved in any crimes. Whatever happened took place before I was born. I've never heard of any theft connected to my grandparents, but somehow I shouldn't be surprised.

"What do you want me to do?" I ask.

"Nothing for now," he says, "but we understand your mother is still alive and living at Silver Belles."

"Yes."

"Can we talk to her?"

"I suppose, but she has dementia."

"We'll be in touch."

CHAPTER 3

I have about two hours to kill in between a doctor's appointment downtown and the time I need to pick up my grandkids from school. I decide to go on a joy ride around the "Ville," as we locals call it.

It's been eons since I've had the luxury of time to reminisce about my hometown. I'm now both a widow and a retired teacher so I need not feel guilty for feeling nostalgic. Downtown Steubenville is abuzz with lots of musical history buffs in town for the annual 3-day Dean Martin Festival that begins tomorrow. Banners and swag are draped all over town. Vendors are hawking wares. Restaurants are greeting hungry out-of-towners. The city is popping with activity.

On every street corner you can hear the lilt of Dean's musical stylings, including "That's Amore, Lay Some Happiness on Me, and Everybody Loves Somebody Sometimes". That last title is engraved on Dean's crypt in LA's Westwood Cemetery.

I drive down South Seventh Street past St. Anthony Catholic Church. Dean's immigrant parents, Gaetano (Guy) and Angela

Crocetti, were married there in 1917. Two years later, their son, Dino Paul Crocetti, was born. Guy Crocetti's barber shop was located on Sixth Street My immigrant grandparents and Gracie lived in this neighborhood when Aunt Bee was born. She was baptized at St. Anthony's and had her First Communion there. They moved to another part of town after that.

    I turn and drive down Market Street—the beating heart of my blue-collar birthplace. There are three nearby bridges that cross the Ohio River and connect us with West Virginia. The primary structure was built in 1857 under the name First Panhandle Bridge. Now everyone simply calls it 'the railroad bridge.' The second one is the Market Street Bridge built in 1905 and known as the Steubenville Bridge. The third is the Veterans' Memorial Bridge completed in 1990. As I approach the Market Street Bridge, I gaze at the site where the old railroad depot once stood at Market and Sixth Street The railroad was once vital to these parts. It connected the city with the vast greatness of America. Coal mines dotted Appalachia, and cargo trains bulging with black diamonds—king coal—rolled over the Ohio River and on through towns, traveling to energy plants scattered throughout the region. The first vein of coal was found in Steubenville in 1829. Just as the crashing waves of the sea are music to a sailor's ears, so are the sounds of rumbling coal cars to a miner's ears.

    The Pennsylvania Railroad operated a main line through town and stopped at the passenger station. The famous Spirit of St. Louis was among the trains that rocked and swayed from the Big Apple to the home of the blues. From there passengers could hop another line and head west. The Pennsylvania Railroad ended passenger service to Steubenville in 1971. Before that, freight and passenger stations could be found throughout eastern Ohio in places like Piney Fork, Port Homer, and Mingo Junction.

Further east one block once stood the giant Hub Department Store at Market and Fifth Street This area was once like Disneyland to me. I saw my first beggar brushing his behind against the wall near the entrance to the Hub. We couldn't go to Marshall Fields in Chicago or Bloomingdale's in New York City, but we could go to the Hub—the biggest department store north of Wheeling. When I asked Grandma Viviana why the raggedy man was holding out a cup, she told me to "hush" and give thanks for my blessings.

Across from the Hub were S.S. Kresge and F.W. Woolworth—both of which were meccas for my high school friends, where we spent idle hours eating ice cream sundaes and shopping for notions. The next street over is Fourth Street, which is the site of the annual Rat Pack Parade during the festival. I never miss it and plan on taking Max and Olivia to join in the fun this year.

I glance at the river along State Route 7—also known as Dean Martin Boulevard. Steubenville owes its origin to the Native Americans, frontiersmen, and fur trappers who used their canoes for traveling. The Ville was established in 1797 just 10 years after the new US government created the Northwest Territories. The first city in the new territory was Marietta, Ohio, established in 1788 and named for Marie Antoinette. It is the oldest city in Ohio and the first official American settlement in the Northwest Territory. Marietta, which also sits along the Ohio River, is a mere 114 miles south of here as the river flows.

I look over toward the Market Street Bridge and think of its history. When this structure was built in the early twentieth century, it was used by moonshiners for deliveries and escapes. In those years, Steubenville had a gritty, backwoods reputation, and the men who didn't fuel themselves with beer after work enjoyed a few kicks of 'shine. By 1919, the town's population was 22,000 people comprised mostly of Italian and German working-class folks. Steubenville could boast of 100 saloons and 23 barber shops.

It's hard to say when moonshine was first produced along the Ohio River, but bootleg business in hooch thrived for decades. Today, federal law prohibits individuals from producing distilled spirits at home. If you want to make homemade 'shine, you need a license from the state. As a nod to the past, New Straitsville, Ohio, in Perry County has a Moonshine Festival every year.

I look across the river at Weirton, West Virginia. In its heyday Steubenville businesses and the Jefferson County Courthouse provided jobs for nearby residents of the Mountain State. When the steel industry started to decline, Weirton became more diversified with retail and medical services. Weirton is most famous as a film location for the Robert DeNiro and Meryl Streep movie *The Deer Hunter*. Novelist Ellery Queen also spent time in Weirton while researching his novel *The Egyptian Cross Mystery*.

I realize I still have a half hour before I pick up the kids. I make a swing back to Market Street and think about how Steubenville once had four fabulous theatres. The Olympic Theatre on Market Street opened in 1916. The Grand Theatre building, located on Fourth Street, was built in 1885 as a saloon, restaurant, and livery stable. In the 1920s, new owners converted it into an auditorium with Vaudeville acts and silent movies. The Grand was followed by the Paramount Theatre in 1931. It was located on Fifth Street and was home to the Mighty Wurlitzer organ. The Paramount played films by RKO. The Capitol Theatre, also on Fourth Street, opened in 1925 and had a Morton organ. It showed mostly Warner Brothers films. Of those four, only the Grand still exists and is owned by the Steubenville Historic Landmarks Foundation. It is in the process of being renovated.

I always feel a twinge of nostalgia when I drive down Market Street. Big G's Cigar Store was nestled among the retail establishments on this street. Grandma Viviana's Passages stationery store was around the corner. As I drive along the streets now, it looks like so many other small towns tucked away from the big urban areas of Ohio. We can't seem to fully shake our reputation as a magnet for establishments using false fronts with hidden passages for illegal operations. There was a time when the facades on low-slung buildings were practically the rule, not the exception. With a wink and a nod, you could partake in just about every illegal activity. Sin was big business. (Hollywood's next gangster TV mini-series should be *Law and Order: Steubenville*.)

I take no pleasure in knowing my grandfather contributed to Steubenville's reputation for vices. Those times are past. The facts are that I never knew my father, but I loved my grandfather. He helped provide a solid childhood for me. My father was murdered before I was born, but it never kept me from leading a normal life. Now that I am retired, my goal is to figure out who murdered my father and why.

I head west on Sunset Boulevard to Stanton Drive. Edwin Stanton is another native son. He was President Abraham Lincoln's secretary of war and a US attorney general. A statue of him graces the front of the Jefferson County Courthouse. Steubenville has always been proud of the fact Lincoln visited our town on February 14, 1861, on his way to his inauguration. He gave a speech at the train station. It was Stanton who said of Lincoln after his death, "Now he belongs to the ages."

I come to the Hollywood Shopping Center and decide to stop at the Kroger's grocery store to pick up after-school snacks. On the side wall is a mural that is two-stories tall with four panels depicting the career of Dean Martin. Among the panels are one that depicts Dean and his partner Jerry Lewis and one with Dean and his Rat Pack buddies. Dean brought Jerry to Steubenville in 1950 and hosted a press conference to drum up publicity for their movies. The town officials then hosted a testimonial dinner in the Fort Steuben Hotel Ballroom—one of Steubenville's grand old structures. The building still stands, but it has been converted into Section 8 housing.

Fans often make pilgrimages to see the mural. Sure enough, I see Gracie's friends Charisse Duhamel and Chip Hanover pointing up at the panels and reminiscing. Charisse is Gracie's lifelong friend and is like a second mother to me. Gracie, Charisse, and Chip were all in the same high-school class. Charisse was a cheerleader, and Chip played football for the Big Red. I approach, and both are excited to see me. It is sad to see them now with their gray hair and stooped shoulders, but they have the same enthusiasm for life and are advocates for their river town. Chip owns Hanover's Auto Repair. His son, Mike, was a good friend of my late husband, Anders. Now Mike has taken over his dad's business, and Mike's son, Ralphie, is learning the trade.

Chip and Charisse are waving their arms at the panel with Dean and Jerry. The comedy duo made 16 movies together. "Did you know that I once took Charisse on a date to see one of them

Dean movies at the Grand Theatre?" Chip says with a strong Appalachian drawl.

"I think it was *The Caddy*," Charisse says.

"Right—I clean forgot the name," Chip chuckles. "Whatever it was, I remember I laughed my ass off. Some of them football buddies of mine were in the theatre that night too. God, I miss my old teammates. Some of them were real rascals. We'd sneak some of the local 'shine into Stanton Park. The park had a roller rink too. We'd drink a little and then go skatin'. I almost broke my leg once when I ran into a wall. My parents would have killed me if they knew I was stinkin' drunk."

I asked if the two of them were going to any of the festival activities in Fort Steuben Park.

"No, but Chip and I are thinking of entering the karaoke contest at the Spot during the festival," Charisse jokes. "We're working on a duet of 'That's Amore.'"

The Spot was the place where the teenage Dean Martin was trained by gamblers to become a croupier. It holds a place of honor in Steubenville lore as part of the "cradle of bookmakers." The Spot and the Naples Spaghetti House are a must for Dean fans when they are in town.

"Didn't Dean once declare that Steubenville was no longer Sin City but Coolville?" I ask.

"Gracie, Chip and I were the coolest kids in the Ville," Charisse laughs. "Just ask our classmates. But it didn't matter—we were all just a bunch of river rats."

Something tells me they are hiding information. The Gracie I know is quiet and reserved. I can't picture her as a hipster. I leave them to their memories and head into Kroger.

The ghost of Dean Martin still hovers over this town. Up until 10 years ago, we often celebrated Gracie's birthday at Naples Spaghetti House on North Street. Locals say Dean and his family ate there when they lived in town and when they visited in later life.

Gracie always loved the festival. She hardly ever missed it. Not only did she have most of Dean's albums but some of his daughter Deana's too. They are presently being stored at Bridgette's house. They will stay there too—I don't want them.

It's now time to go pick up the grandkids. The car radio is blasting the rock band Queen's "Bohemian Rhapsody"—one of my '80s favorites.

Is this the real life? Is this just fantasy?

Sometimes I wonder if I really know the difference.

CHAPTER 4

I'm on a personal mission today. I jump in the car and head back to the Steubenville library. I find the same information associate I saw a couple days ago and note that her name is Giana.

"Do you have a section on Native American history in Ohio and Pennsylvania?"

"Certainly, follow me," Giana says politely.

I view the array of books and thank her. She turns and says, "I have some material in the back room filing cabinets you can look at." Within minutes she is back with a pile of folders.

"We can't let these leave the library, but you can look at them here," she smiles.

There is a wide variety on display before me. There are two volumes on the history of Jefferson County, one on the county's natural resources and another on eastern Ohio geography. The two I am most interested in are a book on the Native Americans of the region and one on the pioneer families of the area. Some of this I already know, having grown up here and working as a history teacher. Some of it is new to me.

I spend several hours perusing the pages. Most of the time I am not certain what I am trying to find, but I keep plugging along. I have the feeling that there is something in this reference section that my mother was very interested in and that she may have been here many times. It's just a hunch, but my hunches have been very good over the years.

Finally, my eyes get tired, and I want to make a stop at Gracie's house before I call it a day.

• • •

I turn the key to the side door of Gracie's small Mingo Junction home and ease myself into the kitchen. I lived here from age six through high school. The place is small but perfect for Gracie's needs before she became incapacitated. All but a few dishes remain in the cupboard. Her beloved teapot sits on the stove in case I want to make tea. I dearly love to cradle a hot cup of tea in my hands. It calms me when things get crazy.

I check the living room and note I need to trash Gracie's analog TV set. Nobody will want this thing—it's an electronics dinosaur. I pass down a hall to her two bedrooms and one bath. Everything appears to be fine.

I head down into the basement and check the plumbing for the washer, dryer, and hot water heater to make sure nothing is leaking. To the right are shelves filled with Mason jars of veggies that Gracie canned five years before. She was always frugal and didn't mind hard work. Her backyard was a full garden in the summer.

I pass near her one-car garage. There is a rose bush near the door that I gave her 10 years ago for Mother's Day. It is in full bloom with lovely pink blossoms. The garage was built by Grandpa Gino about 40 years ago while I was in college. I step inside and note that Gracie's lawn mower is still in its place thanks to my son-in-law Joe. The garage is empty except for a metal baseball bat in one corner and a doll house in the other. I gave Gracie's car to Bridgette last year.

I approach the doll house and note that it is covered in dust and that I should brush it off. I can't bring myself to get rid of it—three generations of little girls have played with it. But I know the only occupants of its rooms now are the mice that scamper around inside looking for food. Just for old time's sake, I pull it out and peer into its backside. I notice there is a small box tucked into the miniature bedroom. I grab it and feel its weight. It's unusually heavy.

I sit down on the concrete floor and lift the lid. There are ten $20 US Liberty gold coins dated 1925. My mind is reeling. How can this be? If someone knew these coins were here, they could have easily broken into the garage. Did Gracie put them in here? Who else could have done it?

I tuck the box under my arm and lock the garage door. I double-check the lock on the house and head out.

• • •

I drive to Bridgette's house in Steubenville. She is expecting me. I hear music before I even reach the door. Bridgette has loved music since she was a baby. Music lessons for her began at age five. Piano first, then clarinet. Two years later she started playing the violin. At age 15 she picked up a guitar and taught herself—she's a natural. Bridgette followed my husband and me into the education field. After graduation from college, she got a job in the Mingo Junction public middle school where she is the band teacher. She gives private lessons after school.

During her second year of teaching, she married Joe Fellows, who now owns my late husband's electronics store. As a side hustle he deals in antiques. I explain all the latest developments to Bridgette, and she is as perplexed about the events as I am.

"Let's start with the gold coins," Bridgette says. "By the date, grandma probably got those from Big G. Those can't be something she herself would have invested in. I'll have Joe look them over. He has seen rare coins before and can give you a ballpark number based on their worth.

"As far as the garnets go, you're going to need an expert to check those out, providing that the police give them to you," Bridgette says. "They may keep them, darn it. The Indian artifacts are a different matter. The police are never going to give you those, and besides, they should go to a museum. You might want to get an attorney. Joe knows a couple of them through his Lions Club. Then, of course, there is Bennington. He's a good friend of Gracie's and still in practice last I heard."

"That would be helpful," I say. "I don't know what I'm getting into."

"But the Glock—Jesus, that scares me. I doubt the police will hand that thing over to you."

My precious grandson pops into the room fresh from playing with his Legos. "How's Great-Grandma Gracie?" he asks.

"About the same. I'm afraid she's not getting any better."

"Remember when she used to play Hide and Seek with me? She said it was her favorite game."

"Max, I'm afraid it still is," I sigh. "If you only knew."

• • •

There are a hundred things I'd like to do today, and going to Silver Belles is the last place I want to go. I debate with myself on whether to swing by and see Gracie or go shopping. My conscience gets the better of me, and I stop by Gracie's room.

"I want you to take me shopping," Gracie demands. "I need new underwear and some cigarettes."

The nurse's aides change Gracie's adult diapers because she cannot walk and she's incontinent. There's no way on God's green earth that I can get her into a car, let alone take her into a store. I'd rather try and put pajamas on a giraffe than change her wet bedding every other hour.

As for the cigarettes, Gracie would have to be put in a wheelchair by Foley lift with two aides to go outside for a smoke. I insist we must not cater to her addiction. That would be classified not as a 'no,' but a 'hell no!'

I try to pump Gracie for more background information. I ask if Gino ever dealt in antique coins. She replies that he had a friend who did. When I ask his name, she can't remember.

I go to the office and get out my mother's checkbook to pay the bill for another month of care at Silver Belles. Gracie and I set up a joint checking account several years ago, which, thankfully, she readily agreed to. It has made this nursing home mess much easier. Mentally I total all the numbers in her savings account and CDs and know that within the year she will run out of funds unless I sell her house in Mingo Junction. I dread it. Gracie and I lived there from the time I was six until I left for college. All the old neighbors have either died or passed away, yet the memories hover around me every time I drive down her street or step into the house.

I decide to go back to see Gracie once more before I leave the building. She is watching *The Price Is Right.*

"Is it warm enough to go for a bike ride?" she asks.

"It's warm outside, Mom, but I don't think you're strong enough to use the pedals." It's tough pretending that she could ever walk, let alone ride a bike again, but I humor her.

"But I want to go to the baseball lot," she demands. The lot is three blocks from her house, but a convenience store is there now.

"Why?"

"I want to see Toby's game."

Toby. Why did she have to say that? I turn my head so she doesn't see a tear roll down my cheek. Toby was my oldest child—Bridgette's older brother. He dearly loved baseball. When he was eight years old we let him ride his bike to the sandlot baseball field on Gracie's street where the neighborhood kids all played.

On the way home he was carrying a bat that he used to hit a home run. The bat started to slip in his hand and Toby lost his grip. His bike veered into the street and he was hit by a car. He died two days later.

I tell Gracie I need to leave and will see her tomorrow. I get in the car and shove a CD of Mozart's music into the player. Before I reach home *Requiem* is playing, and I turn the volume full blast. Two seconds later the windshield is a blur and I pull over to the side of the road. Ten minutes pass without me moving a muscle. I gather myself together and drive the last 200 feet to my house. I'm exhausted, and I vow to go straight to bed.

• • •

It's a pleasant day for a drive to Beaver Falls, Pennsylvania. I have no idea what I am doing or why I am doing it, but I'm going. Gracie had mentioned Beaver Falls and something about a roadhouse, so why not drive there for a perfect summer joy ride.

The town is 35 miles north of Pittsburgh, with rolling hills and lots of trees. I like driving alone along country roads in the daytime but would never do it at night. I watch too many scary crime dramas on TV, and my imagination is too active. I think about all the times Gracie and I used to watch 1980's cop shows ("Be careful out there." *Hill Street Blues*).

I cross the Beaver Falls town limits sign (population 9,005) and head downtown. Before I left home I put the address of the Carnegie Free Library on my cell phone, and I soon find the building. I head straight to the information desk, where a pleasant young man in a Pittsburgh Pirates t-shirt smiles at me.

"I'm a teacher from Ohio, and I'm trying to learn about the community here," I say. "Do you have a section on local history?"

"Sure, I'll show you," he smiles. I like the fact he's a Pirates fan—I'm sure he's acquainted with Captain Morgan, my favorite pirate.

He leads me to a stack of assorted booklets, old high-school yearbooks, maps of city and state parks, church directories, and assorted evidence that the town was founded in 1868. I thank him for his help and ask, "There used to be a roadhouse outside of town that was popular in the 1950s. I believe they had dancing on weekends. Do you know of it?"

"No, ma'am, sorry." He wanders off.

I spend an hour knee-deep in local history and discover there used to be lots of mining in the area. I am not surprised—coal is mined in eastern and southern Ohio and throughout the Appalachians. One thing, however, jumped out of the page at me—the Keystone Driller Company.

The Keystone Driller Company existed in Beaver Falls from 1891–1959. They sold all kinds of products, including the Keystone Driller tractor and the Keystone gold finder. I see from the information there was another area company that manufactured steel plates for the US Bureau of Engraving and Printing. Could Jefferson or Carlton have stolen a currency plate in Beaver Falls and trafficked it to Grandpa Gino?

I gather up my notes, satisfied with the info I have found. As I turn to leave, I run into the information associate with a broad pirate's grin on his face.

"Hey, I want to tell you that I called my mom and asked her if there had ever been a roadhouse outside of town," he says. "She said there was one on Victory Road, but it's been torn down. It had quite a reputation."

"Just out of curiosity," I ask, "what was its name?"

"The Gold Mine."

"Do you have any old newspapers on microfilm?"

"Sure, the *Beaver County Times*. They are over there," he points.

I start rolling through microfilm starting in January of 1958. It doesn't take long to find a box advertisement for the place.

The Gold Mine—Home of the Driller.
Dancing Every Friday & Saturday - 8 p.m. to 1 a.m.
Adult Beverages. Largest dance floor in town.
Can you 'Dig It'?

I laugh. Gracie used to talk about the beatniks' vernacular used back in the late '50s. She loved watching '50s-era TV shows like *Dobie Gillis* and *77 Sunset Strip*. I've got new ammo to aim at Gracie. Maybe I can jar some memories loose.'

• • •

Beatnik: a person who participated in a social movement of the 1950s and early 1960s which stressed artistic self-expression and the rejection of the mores of conventional society.

From everything I've ever read, the Beat Generation was full of intellectuals who were reacting against institutional American values and conformity. They loved the cool jazz of Dizzy Gillespie and Miles Davis, and the writings of Jack Kerouac (*On The Road*). They also had a deep connection with the poetry of Allen Ginsberg (*Howl*) and Lawrence Ferlinghetti (*A Coney Island of the Mind*).

As I make my dinner I search my brain for any time Gracie has mentioned beatniks. I've never seen a photo of her in a beret, but I do know she likes jazz in addition to big band and '50s crooners like Dean Martin. Somewhere in the back of my mind I remember hearing that Steubenville had a beatnik coffeehouse for a time. Places like that had poetry readings and guitar music but usually didn't stay in business long, especially in small towns.

I work up enough courage to call Charisse Duhamel. Gracie was always closer to Charisse than she was to her own sister, my Aunt Bee. Charisse is very worried about Gracie and calls me once a week. We chat and then I zero in on my big question. "Was there ever a coffeehouse in town during the '50s? A place where poetry was read?"

"Oh, sure, honey," Charisse says sweetly. "Your mom and I went a few times. She dabbled in poetry for a while—lots of us did. We would listen to jazz records at my house and scribble in our notebooks. It kept us out of trouble."

"But did you ever go to the coffeehouse?"

"A few times. Some cute fellas hung out there. It was popular for about a year, then it fizzled out. I think Big G invested in it but lost some money. It wasn't too far from his cigar store."

I thank Charisse and promise continuing updates on Gracie's health. Now I'm even more confused. A new picture is emerging of my mother.

My iPhone rings, and I see it is Bridgette. "Mom, I've got something you might find interesting."

"I'm all ears."

"I was taking a photo out of an old frame that Grandma Gracie had once given me, and I found a document folded up behind it." Bridgette hesitates for a second then takes a deep breath. "It says Carlton Bergstrom purchased 400 shares of stock in something called Barton Mines of Johnsburg, New York."

CHAPTER 5

I pull my car into the parking lot next to a sign that says *Attorney Benington Southwick—Appointments Only*. Ben is an old family friend and someone I can trust. After exchanging pleasantries, I get right to the point.

"Bridgette found this document behind one of Gracie's picture frames," I begin.

I prattle on about the stock and the fact my father's cousin apparently purchased it. Ben well knows the rumors that Carlton Bergstrom may have poisoned my father. I mention the garnet ring that I found, the postcard from the Barton Mine, the jeweled bracelet, and the New York license plates. I also mention I'd really like to know more about Carlton and Jefferson. I purposely don't mention the Glock or the small bag of garnets the police are keeping.

"I'll check out this document, Mo," he says, using my nickname. "It's very odd since Gracie never speaks about your father or his cousin. Maybe the document is legit, but I'm suspicious."

I hop back in my car and head to the grocery store. Gracie wanted some special cookies, and I need a loaf of bread. As I'm rolling my cart down the liquor aisle, my iPhone rings. I recognize the name on the caller ID.

"Mrs. Albrecht, this is Tim Konig from the Steubenville Police—you know, your old student."

"Yes, of course." I try to sound cheery. He's calling from his personal phone. I lean up against the shelf to my right and see a variety of rum bottles. One of them is Captain Morgan. I swear that pesky pirate is winking straight at me, begging me to take a drink.

"An old building on Fourth Street has been sold and is being renovated," Tim begins. "The workers have made an interesting discovery."

He explains that the owner died and the building's top floor had not been used since the late 1950s. "When the workers got to that floor, the door was locked and they had to break it down," he explained. "The inside of the room was like passing through a time machine. There were newspapers from 1959, pool tables, and card tables with decks still sitting on them. The bar was stocked with old Rolling Rock pony bottles. I'm calling you because there was one more thing they found: a stack of betting slips with Big G's name on them."

I thank Tim for calling me, hoping he doesn't get in trouble for the "inside" info. I move on three steps, grab two bottles of Merlot (vintage—last month), and head for the cash register while memories of drinking Rolling Rock ponies in high school prance in my head.

. . .

I need to regroup. Suddenly there is so much consternation whirling around. All these thoughts are like planes circling the airport, waiting to land and taxi to a safe zone.

I put on some soothing Celtic music and pull out a setting of my grandmother's good china. Viviana always said tea tastes better in a china cup. I put a place setting down on the kitchen table and set a bowl of Hersey's Kisses in front of me. I have the bright idea to put one silver Kiss on the dinner plate for every new development that has occurred in the last month.

I start with one for my first encounter with the police and one each for the garnet ring, the New York license plate, the Glock, the gold coins, the Beaver Falls roadhouse, the betting slips, the Barton Mines postcard, the Indian artifacts, the diamond bracelet, and the stock. After a moment I add one for the genealogist, one for Carlton Bergstrom's driver's license, one for my second encounter with the police, and one for the call from Tim Konig. That makes 15.

I think about the information associates at the two libraries. I stir my tea and worry about Max and Gracie. My mother is a lost cause—closer to death than she is to life. Max, however, has his whole life in front of him, and we must find doctors who can assist with his autoimmune disease. He is doing well in school and seems to have lots of friends. Furthermore, he and Joe have gotten into radio-controlled airplanes, and they love to go to a friend's farm field outside of town and fly them.

I stare at the kitchen clock and wonder about the Bergstroms—my father and his cousin. Gracie has always refused to talk about my dad. Where did he come from? Why did she marry him? Did she love him? Why didn't my grandparents talk about him?

I grab the *Herald-Star* to see if there's anything new in 'Little Chicago.' There's a photo of kids in the local swimming pool, ads for August back-to-school clothing, and some letters to the editor.

Another story grabs my attention. Under the heading "Steubenville Crime Report," it seems a business owner on Market Street reported to the police their safe was broken into some time over the last week. No checks or cash were stolen. Instead, the perpetrator stole some jewelry that belonged to the owner. Among the missing items was an emerald bracelet and ruby earrings belonging to a deceased relative. I laugh at myself for thinking that this is exactly the kind of heist I suspect Big G's men could have pulled. The legend of Market Street continues.

The phone rings and I see that it is Bridgette. "Hi Mom," she says. "Good news on the gold coins. Joe took one to a pawn broker in Wheeling when he was there on a business run, and the owner said one coin like that is worth more than $2,000. How about that?"

Damn! "The lot of them could be worth $20,000! Tell Joe I owe him a dinner."

Maybe things are looking up.

• • •

I'm in the car with Bridgette, Max, and Olivia on a day trip to Beaver Falls. I told Bridgette we should squeeze in a joy ride before the kids go back to school in two weeks. Bridgette is driving and I'm navigating. I am still in awe that a cell phone can guide you to places via GPS. It proves you CAN teach an old dog new tricks!

I tell the grandkids that we are going to see a lot of beavers on this trip, and they laugh.

"We're going to Beaver County along the Beaver River and the Beaver Trail to get to Beaver Falls," I say.

"What are we going to do there? Build a dam?" Max asks.

"No, we're just going to have fun—no work. We'll stop first at Buttermilk Falls and then head south to Beaver Falls Historical Museum. After that we'll eat Beaver pizza."

They laugh harder—they know I am kidding, but only partially. I've discovered there is a cute little pizza shop on Seventh Avenue called D&G Pizza, and they will love it.

We navigate to Route 18 just south of the Pennsylvania Turnpike and find our way to Buttermilk Falls. There's a trail right off the parking lot with an easy walk to the falls. The kids have never seen a waterfall so they are enthralled. We take another path and come to a spot where the water is practically in our faces. The kids giggle and threaten to throw each other in, but I know they're kidding. Bridgette is lucky that her children get along well and are curious about everything.

After a half-hour of sightseeing, we pile back into the car and head downtown. We pull into the Beaver Falls Historical Society and Museum on Seventh Avenue and head inside. The kids know that I will be teaching them something about history. I try to take every opportunity to do so.

We enter and are soon absorbed into the displays. I've done my homework in preparation for this trip, and soon I'm explaining that Delaware Indians once lived in this area in the mid to late 1700s.

"Around 1750 a Moravian missionary named David Zeisberger settled in Lawrence County, Pennsylvania, for a while.

His mission was to convert Native Americans like the Seneca and Delaware tribes to Christianity. Some of the Delaware invited him and his followers to explore their territory. They got into canoes and followed the Mahoning River to the Beaver River to what is today Beaver Falls," I explain.

The kids giggle again at the mention of more beavers, but I can tell they are interested. We view some Native American artifacts before going on to other exhibits.

Among the displays is one on how Pennsylvania is known as the producer of plates for US currency. Congress established the Philadelphia Mint in 1792. In the back of my mind, I remember reading about the garnet mines of New York and how the gems are used to make plates to produce currency. Could there be a connection?

There is no time to think about any other displays because the kids are hungry. We jump in the car and drive to D&G Pizza. Max and Olivia can hardly sit still as they gawk at the pictures on the menu. Max teases Olivia that he wants anchovies on their pizza, so she slugs him on the arm.

"No, that will stink up the whole pizza," she frowns. I agree with her. The kids settle for extra pepperoni. Bridgette and I order a pizza with cheese and onion.

Once we are all stuffed we head back to the car. I've got a favor to ask my daughter.

"On our way back home, I want to route us down Victory Street," I say casually.

"Is that on the way?" Bridgette asks.

"No, but I was here a few weeks ago and there's something I want to show you."

"Okay, Mom," she says. "I didn't know you spent time here."

"I haven't. But Gracie did."

Bridgette looks at me cross-eyed and starts the car. Within a few minutes we're heading down Victory Street on our way back south and out of town. We approach the lot where the Gold Mine once stood. There's a Wegman's grocery store there now.

"Pull over into the parking lot," I say.

"Do you need something in the store?"

"No, I'm trying to feel a certain musical vibe."

"What?" she says with concern in her voice.

"Do you hear a mix of jazz, blues, and folk music in the air?"

"Mom, do you need a doctor?"

I laugh. "I'll tell you about it when we get home."

• • •

It's a lovely late August morning and I decide to run a few errands before stopping to see Gracie. When I get to Silver Belles I find her room empty, so I look around. Gracie can't get out of bed unless two aides use a Foley lift to hoist her up and ease her into a Broda chair. She can't be far.

I ask someone in the nurse's station where Gracie went, and they say to look outside in the garden. Sure enough, Gracie is there looking at the flowers. An aide is by her side.

"So, you're out taking a walk," I say, faking a cheery lilt to my voice.

"The flowers are getting ready to die, and so am I," Gracie replies.

"The flowers look good, Mom. They are getting plenty of sun and water."

"It's almost September, and by the end of the month they'll be dead. The flowers are better off than I am. At least they are outside."

I try to think of something to cheer her up. I come up short.

"What can I get for you?"

"I want a cigarette and a highball," Gracie demands. "Make it snappy!"

It's rare to see Gracie this depressed. I tell her I will drive down the street and pick her up a strawberry milkshake—her favorite. I also mention I'll try to bring Max and Olivia over to see her tomorrow.

It works. Gracie forces a slight smile and I scoot out.

• • •

I promised Bridgette that I would tell her about Gracie's outings to the Gold Mine, but there was no time yesterday when we got home. The grandkids were tired and just wanted to play on their electronic devices, and Bridgette had some lesson plans to work on. School will be starting next week.

Bridgette has her teapot boiling when I arrive. It is hot out today, and the kids are outside playing in the sprinkler. They tell me they are going in the family's RV this weekend on a trip to Wheeling to see Joe's elderly grandparents. They left some cookies on the table for me. I head inside.

"I told them you were coming, and they wanted you to have a treat," Bridgette says. "What's this about Grandma Gracie and the musical vibes. Sounds crazy."

I start by telling Bridgette that the more I go through Gracie's personal effects, the more I discover her earlier life.

"I thought I understood her better, but it turns out not to be the case," I start. "There's parts of her life we didn't know about—and I'm not just talking about Jefferson and Carlton Bergstrom."

"I'm intrigued, Mom," Bridgette says. "What have you uncovered?"

"There's a list, but I'll start with a place called the Gold Mine in Beaver Falls."

I tell Bridgette that I suspect Gracie spent time in Beaver Falls from something she let slip one day. She seemed all too familiar with a roadhouse south of town. I reveal I called Gracie's friend Charisse and asked if the two of them had ever visited a roadhouse when they were in their late teens.

"What did Charisse say?" Bridgette says, eager for an answer.

I explain that Charisse seemed to have fond memories of listening to jazz and blues at the Beaver Falls roadhouse as well as one that used to be in Steubenville. Apparently the local one was more of a coffeehouse where poetry was read.

"I can't imagine Grandma Gracie would do that. So do you suppose she wrote her own poems?"

"I'll let you know if I find any. She always liked to read, and she spent a lot of time in Aunt Bee's library. Charisse let me know recently that she and Gracie considered themselves "hipsters" during high school. Very strange. I feel there is a part of Gracie that we don't know about."

"Like why she married Jefferson? We don't even know where he came from or where his cousin went after Jefferson died. What is Gracie hiding?"

"I'm trying to find out. Some of this feels very unsettling to me. I need to pump Charisse for more information. I must get her in the right mood."

...

I get an unsolicited call from a real estate agent asking me if I want to sell my house. I don't, of course, but it gets me thinking. I need to put Gracie's house on the market, but I've been dreading it. There are still some things I need to clean out, like the attic and Gracie's desk. Most of the basement has already been emptied thanks to Joe's help.

I hop in the car and head to Mingo Junction. I figured I'd treat myself to a double cheeseburger after doing some cleaning. Tomorrow I'll eat healthy—I swear to myself.

It's the first day of school for the grandkids, and you can tell the air has a slight change to it. I remember how much I loved the first day of school and seeing friends I hadn't seen all summer. There was also the thrill of wearing some new clothes my mother bought in either Steubenville's Hub Department Store or on a rare trip to the mall in Wheeling. She had a coffee can on her dresser where she would put her spare change. Each August she would count it out and use it to buy my new clothes.

Gracie's house is enveloped in bright sun and blue sky. The maple leaves on the tree in her front yard still exude bright green. In two months, they will be so brittle they will fall to the ground. It's the circle of life. A neighbor walking her dog waves as I unlock the side door. It's a scene of true Americana except the owner of the house will never live here again.

I enter the kitchen and make a mental note I need to dispose of the painting of a rooster that hangs on the wall. I painted it in fifth grade when Viviana bought me an artist's kit for Christmas. I was no Rembrandt—more like Salvador Dali after three drinks. But Gracie loved it.

My mission today is to clean out Gracie's desk. I start throwing pens, paper clips, and notepads in a box. There are a few handmade Christmas cards from the twins and a few receipts and flyers. Another drawer is full of instruction manuals for various appliances long since deposited in the landfill. Under the pile is a yellowed envelope. On the front are two words—Gold Mine.

The note is in cursive and had obviously been hand-delivered. I carefully open the envelope. The writing is impeccable but there is not a date. It is a poem.

It was signed 'C.'

CHAPTER 6

Bridgette has asked me to pull out a couple of old photo albums so Olivia and Max can begin to learn about their ancestors. Olivia, for one, is anxious for me to tell her the history of the Rivers family in Steubenville.

I'm glad the twins are starting to show an interest in their hometown. Most kids aren't that self-aware at age eight. I will rehearse the stories I want to tell them without getting too deep into the weeds. There has been a concerted effort in Steubenville over the last 50 years to plant flowers among those weeds without totally disowning the city's past. Hopefully the twins' generation will not put upon themselves the 'river rat' moniker that was so prominent during Gracie's life. I'm willing to discuss some of Big G's activities when the twins are in their teens, but right now I want them to know how tough it was for an Italian immigrant family to come to America and put down new roots.

Viviana was born in the Naples area of Italy in 1915. Little is known to me about her parents, Arturo and Rosa Tattini, and their lives in Italy before marriage. She knew her father worked on the docks and her mother worked as *la cameriera* (house maid). They shared a small apartment with another couple, and life was very simple.

Viviana passed along a few things she knew about her birthplace, but she was only three when her parents booked passage for New York. The biggest thing she remembered was the smokestack on the ship and the loud blasts of the horn as they approached the Statue of Liberty. She remembered her arrival came on an idyllic blue-sky day. She recalled being so excited that she jumped up and down at the sight of Lady Liberty and accidentally peed her pants.

Arturo and Rosa only spoke Italian at home so Viviana was at a great disadvantage when she went to public school three years after arriving in Steubenville. Her parents had poor English skills so they enlisted a retired teacher from their church to help. Viviana became a good student but dropped out of high school during the Depression to take a job as a cook in a local Italian restaurant. It was while working there that she met my grandfather Gino.

Gino's parents and an uncle also came to America from the Calabria area of Italy a few years before Viviana's family. The Calabria region is the "toe" of Italy's peninsula, which is full of rugged mountains and crystal-clear beaches. There is a decidedly Greek influence on the area, with people who love a robust cuisine. One of their favorite foods is a spicy sausage called Nduja ,made with locally grown chiles.

Unfortunately, a mafia-type organization called the Ndrangheta developed in the impoverished sections of the Calabria region during the nineteenth century. They were known for loan sharking and racketeering, among other pursuits. They heavily relied on traditional clan or family loyalties to run their operations. Gino's parents, like Viviana's, wanted to go to America to start a new life. The Flusso surname was quickly changed to Rivers at Ellis Island, and eventually they landed in Steubenville, where Gino's father and uncle found jobs as bouncers in local saloons. A few years later they found better paying jobs in the steel mill. Gino Gabriele Rivers was born in 1913, weighing almost nine pounds. His parents were very proud to call their new son an American and guessed that he could become a future prize fighter like the reigning national champion, Jack Johnson.

Gino was not particularly fond of school. Often he and his cousin Sal would get into fights in their neighborhood as the boys fought for their territory. By age 16, Gino had dropped out of school and started working for the owner of Smitty's Card Shop, where lovely young ladies assisted customers while they played poker and shot pool. By age 23, Smitty had left town with another man's wife, and Gino received a bargain basement offer to purchase the establishment.

Gino met Viviana late one afternoon as he went to eat an early supper before working the late shift at Smitty's. Viviana had come out of the kitchen to assist one of the waitresses, and Gino spotted her. Soon he was engaging her in conversation and asked if she would like to go on a day off to Stanton Park and ride the merry-go-round. She accepted, and a year later they were married.

As a child, I simply adored Gino. Whenever I entered his store after school or during summer break his face would burst into smiles. His wit was as sharp as a bowie knife and his memory even sharper. His physique was as broad as a barn, but every man in Steubenville knew Gino could knock them down with a knuckle sandwich.

He had a gentle side too. He would offer to walk me over to Woolworth's to get ice cream or take me to an afternoon kid's movie at one of the local downtown theatres. When I was 13, I wanted him to take me to see *The Godfather*. Instead, we went to see the Disney classic *The Jungle Book*. It took me years to realize why he passed on Don Vito Corleone and opted for Shere Khan and Baloo instead.

Since I knew nothing about my father, I looked to Gino as my protector. He was always around to help Grace and me with a problem. He also protected Viviana from hoodlums who mistakenly wanted to take over her business. She could be as tough as nails if she had to be, but it helped to have Gino and his trusted employees in her corner.

As much as I adored Gino, there was the other man in my life—Anders. I first saw Anders during my junior year of high school when he had a small part in his senior class play. I attended the show with a girlfriend who had a mad crush on the lead actor. I didn't think much about it then. I had plenty of other things on my mind, such as the fact the first *Star Wars* movie had become a craze and the Apple II computer with two floppy disk drives had come onto the market. Meanwhile, Gracie was fretting about the energy crisis even though our corner Sohio station was selling gas for 65 cents a gallon. As for Charisse, the worst thing she could ever imagine—the death of Elvis—had her in a blue funk for months.

I didn't meet Anders until my freshman year of college. I was in line at a Roy Rogers fast-food restaurant near campus, and he was standing next to me. Something possessed me to tap him on the shoulder and say "Howdy, partner," as Roy (King of the Cowboys) would have said on his TV show. Anders stared at me for a moment and then laughed. I quickly croaked out "I'm from Mingo Junction," and soon we were eating Double R-Bar burgers together. We chatted about Roy and the fact he was born Leonard Slye in Cincinnati but grew up in a little speck of nowhere called Duck Run, north of Portsmouth. He asked me if I needed a ride home for Thanksgiving break and gave me his phone number.

We rode together a couple of times but didn't go on an actual date until early spring. I felt we really bonded over the strangest of discussions—hair-metal rock bands. Anders was into Led Zeppelin and Def Leopard. I was not fond of metal but confessed I could tolerate Deep Purple and Jethro Tull. It was the craziest conversation as we ran through each band's playlist. The minute he finished his analysis of Zeppelin's "Kashmir," I knew Anders was someone special.

We got married right after I graduated from college. Anders was already teaching biology at Steubenville High School. I started teaching history as well as the dreaded health class all teenagers hated. At least I could ask Anders, the biology teacher, detailed questions about zygotes and gametes even though we rarely discussed that in class.

We named our first car Nellybelle, of course, and our first dog was a German shepherd named Bullet. Roy Rogers would have been proud of us. Anders and I would challenge each other with quirky questions such as 'Why do the British eat baked beans for breakfast?' and 'Has Queen Elizabeth II ever tasted Skittles?'

We raised Bridgette and Toby in a quiet neighborhood and always had Sunday dinner with Gracie in Mingo Junction. Anders spent quality time with each child but never delayed correcting them if they did something wrong. For example, Anders patiently played with Bridgette as she moved pieces all through her doll house but corrected her when she enlisted the dog to help clean food off the dishes. He took Toby out fishing and camping but corrected him when he took a book of US postage stamps and stuck them all over the living room window.

We took a few family excursions together when the kids were small, once driving all the way to Cincinnati to see a Reds baseball game. Toby loved the enormous stadium but kept asking why the players spit all the time. Anders had no good answer. Toby said he would never do that when he, himself, got to the big leagues.

When Toby was seven, Anders resumed his old hobby of flying radio-controlled airplanes as he had with his childhood friend Mike Hanover. Toby was fascinated with flight and decided maybe he would go into the air force someday. Then the unthinkable tragedy struck us all with Toby's death, and we, as a family, could have become unhinged. We looked to Anders to guide us. He was very stoic and held himself, and us, together. We grudgingly moved forward.

The years passed, and Anders was so proud the day he walked Bridgette down the aisle as she married Joe. Anders became ill with cancer around the time of the twins' first birthday, and Joe stepped up to run the electronics store. Shortly after the twins' fourth birthday, Anders died. I miss him every day, especially when tensions are growing. I'm not certain how my pursuit of finding my father's murderer is going to end, but I do know that Anders is watching over me.

CHAPTER 7

Every fall I take my car to Hanover's Auto Repair for its annual checkup. Mike Hanover was a childhood friend of my late husband, and I taught his son Ralphie in school. Ralphie is slowly taking over the repair business just as Mike took over the operation from his father, Chip Hanover. Ralphie is a good athlete, who also plays on the same softball team as my son-in-law Joe. The Hanovers are reliable and run the best repair shop in town. They are like family.

The car shop is only a few doors down from the Steubenville library, and my normal routine is to leave the vehicle for a couple hours and go browse the stacks.

Today I have mining on my mind. Gracie has left too many clues about her interest in mining, between the Barton Mines in New York and the Keystone Driller Company in Beaver Falls. I don't yet know what to think about the Gold Mine roadhouse. I'll pursue that later.

I dig into research on the Keystone Driller Company. It was founded by two brothers—Robert and John Downie—in 1879 in western Pennsylvania. Their steam-powered rig was a favored oil drilling machine of its day.

Another part of their business centered around manufacturing prospecting machines for coal, zinc, lead, and, most interestingly, gold. Competition in this field at the time was quite brisk, but the Keystone gold finder and the Keystone Driller tractor appeared to lead the pack.

The brothers first plant was in Fallston on the west side of the Beaver River. Later the plant moved up to Beaver Falls.

I find a 1903 article from *The Beaver Times* with the headline "Keystone Driller Company Ships Machine Far Away." The article states one of their big drilling machines would be sent to Sixty Mile Creek, Alaska. "It will be shipped over the Pittsburgh and Lake Erie Railroad and will go via Dawson City."

I keep looking through research material and run across a book published by Keystone in 1920 entitled *Klondike: The Chicago Records Book for Gold Seekers*. It states, "Everything which a gold seeker should know that can be placed in type is contained in this book."

It appears the Keystone gold finder was a hot commodity at one point in the 1920s. Between the years 1923–1945, Keystone employed 400 workers. Nibbling at the back of my mind is the thought that somehow Steubenville folks could have a connection to a town an hour's drive away. Could two of those folks have been Big G and Jefferson Bergstrom?

. . .

The car has been running like a top, as Gracie used to say, and I decide to stop at the Fort Steuben Mall to purchase a new floor lamp to put next to my reading chair. My comfy chair is like an old friend—I feel most relaxed there. I hope it never wears out. I pull into the parking lot and Bridgette calls. She needs me to watch Olivia after school so she can take Max to get new glasses.

"Please tell Olivia she needs to practice her piano. She has a lesson tomorrow," Bridgette says.

I love spending time with the grandkids. Olivia is a bright and creative child but sensitive like her mother. She loves music (ditto Mom) and is taking piano lessons. She tells me her goal is to learn violin so she and Bridgette can play a duet. Along with her music, Olivia loves art. I marvel at how she can draw plants and animals better than many teenagers I've known.

I contemplate the progression of music throughout the lives of the women in my family. Viviana (born in 1920) grew up in a household with a Victrola. Gracie (born in 1939) was raised in a home with a 1930s Crosley tube radio. I (born in 1960) had a portable record player as a teenager that spun LPs and 45 rpm records and later graduated to an eight-track cartridge tape player (coolest thing in town!). Bridgette (born in 1982) had a Walkman cassette player with headphones. She wanted a boom box but Anders nixed it. Olivia (born in 2014) has wireless headsets, and I'm certain she'll have a cell phone with Spotify, or something similar, in a couple years.

I continue to be amazed at Olivia's childhood as opposed to mine. She has a loving father who is kind and supportive. Her mother is both creative and grounded. With luck, she'll never know about Steubenville's seamy history.

I don't want my grandchildren to be tainted by the gambling, bootlegging, and prostitution that once permeated Steubenville. I don't want them to feel hurt when someone refers to the eastside of Mingo Junction as the 'Bottoms.' Most of all I don't want them to know about the Black Hand extortion that once cast dark shadows on my hometown. How do I stop that?

Olivia and Max will be preteens in a couple years and then full-fledged teenagers in an age of cell phone madness. When I was a preteen, I went through the summer of 1970 (the 'Summer of Love') that I call the 'Barbie-to-Beatles-to-Books' phase of my life. Gracie had given me a Barbie doll when I was six. I played with it only when a classmate who lived on my street invited me over. She had Barbie's Dream House and a Barbie car, which Gracie thought were way too frivolous an expense. I tried not to be jealous. By that summer I was burnt out on Barbie and was moving on.

I had another friend that year who shared my interest in the Beatles. She liked Paul. I liked Ringo. Everyone had a favorite back then—even my Aunt Bee was a fan of George (the cerebral one, she said).

My friend and I went to see the documentary *Let It Be* and cried when we heard the Beatles were breaking up. I was certain my world was coming to an end.

And then came the books. I immersed myself in history. I had no idea that the books would lead me to my life's work, but I knew I loved learning about our nation's rebellion against the British and the rise of the USA to becoming the world's strongest power and a beacon of hope. Reading Mary Lazarus's poem on the Statue of Liberty opened my eyes and led me to try and learn as many details as my brain could hold. I want my grandkids to know America—warts and all. But I want them to know that Steubenville is still developing into something better than its past.

Olivia was practicing her next piece (Beethoven's "Fur Elise") when I was knocked back from deep thoughts by my cell phone ringing. Once again, it was the Steubenville police.

"Mrs. Albrecht, Sergeant Gambino would like for you to stop by tomorrow."

"I'll be there."

• • •

My idea of absolute hell is to be stuck in an elevator next to a man smoking a stinky cigar. As I pull into the parking lot of the police station, I vow I would transport myself to that very elevator as penance for my sins if it meant I didn't have to go into the building again and face Gambino. I lumber down the hallway sucking on two antacid tablets.

I spot my former student Tim Konig.

"You can't stay away, hey Mrs. A?" he laughs. "That sentence rhymes."

"You're a comedian, Tim," I try to smile.

"Sarge will be right in. Make yourself comfortable."

Sure, comfortable. A bed of nails would be nicer. I take a deep breath and await Sergeant Gambino. To try and calm myself I envision Gambino dressed as a pirate in a drag show. I also wonder if I should shutter my agnostic religious tendencies, lay prostate on the floor in front of a priest, beg forgiveness, and promise to attend Mass.

"Mrs. Albrecht, it's nice to see you again," Sergeant Gambino begins. "I have something for you."

The officer opens a filing cabinet drawer and pulls out a cotton bag. With great flair he pulls open the drawstring and spills the contents—Big G's Glock. It lands with a dull thud on the desk. I almost scream.

"The judge released this weapon and said your family could have it back."

I freeze. I hate guns.

"It's okay. We've double-checked it. There are no bullets."

I stick the bag in my purse and sign a document Gambino shoves at me.

"Can I leave now?" I beg.

"Sure, we'll let you out the back door."

They did not give me the bag of garnets.

. . .

I go to my kitchen table and pull the Glock out of the cotton bag and hold it in my hands. I can immediately see why people describe it as 'cold hard steel.' I'm so unsettled I rationalize that it once belonged to Big G and was probably used for protection, but I'm not certain. I know so little about my grandfather's business dealings in his blind tiger establishment and the sordid characters who hung out in the back room. If Gracie knew much of anything, she never said.

I toss and turn all night knowing I have a gun in the house. I worry that the grandkids will find it. Silky gets so pissed at me that she goes and hides in another room. I doze off but around

3:00 a.m. I dream that Captain Morgan is winking at me again—enticing me to get out of bed and mix a drink. I don't budge.

At 4:00 a.m. I go through a cycle where I think I should keep the gun for a while. After all, I am alone in the house, and you never know when someone will try to break in. Maybe a better idea would be to get a German shepherd to protect me, but how would Silky like that?

At 5:30 a.m. I make up my mind that I will take the bag to my bank and put the weapon in my safe-deposit box. I get up and make a pot of coffee. I still have over three hours to kill before the bank opens.

• • •

I am ready to put my plan into action. I'm standing in line waiting for a teller to let me into the vault. As I hot-foot back and forth, I spot Charisse.

"Hi honey," she says excitedly. "You're up early today."

I stammer out an excuse without revealing why it is important to make this early visit to the bank. As she pummels me with questions about Gracie, my palms and feet start to sweat. I hope my discomfort is not showing.

"If you're not in a hurry, why don't we go to the coffee shop next door. You can catch me up with what Bridgette and the kids area doing."

I promise I will meet her in 10 minutes and ask her to get us a table. She scurries off, and I can feel my heart rate going down.

A teller leads me into the vault and leaves. Thankful for the privacy, I open the box and realize I need to make an inventory of all the papers tucked inside. After Anders died, I hired an attorney to settle his estate, then put everything I deemed important in this box.

I'm also storing a few of Gracie's items. She told me she never put much trust in banks—no doubt something Big G and Viviana were leery of too. People who were under the threat of the Black Hand extortion rings don't deal with banks. I make a mental note to bring a stenographer's notebook back in here.

I open the bag and my hands start to shake. For what purpose was this weapon used? Did Big G use it to intimidate the thugs who tried to extort him? Did he ever kill someone? Furthermore, where did it come from? Glocks are German guns, and this gun looks old. I'm not sure Big G served in the military in World War II, let alone if he was in Europe with our fighting forces. Gracie certainly never revealed it if it is true.

• • •

Charisse is in a talkative mood. She and Gracie have remained fast friends since high school. Charisse is divorced with no children. She and Gracie really seem to care for one another, and I look at Charisse as a second mother. She tells me about her trips to Wheeling to visit relatives and to gamble in the casino. She also loves the greyhound racetrack there. Gracie was never one to spend her hard-earned money on slot machines. Sometimes I wonder how Gracie and Charisse stayed so close. Charisse is carefree with a strong independent streak. Gracie always seems burdened.

Our conversation is light and uplifting, and I ponder whether this is finally the right time to ask questions for which I always wanted answers. I am going to go for it.

"Charisse, I know Gracie never speaks of my father, but where did he come from?"

"I can't really say," she says cautiously. "He seemed to just show up in town one day."

"Do you know anything about him?"

Charisse seemed to chew on the inside of her mouth for a minute as if deciding what exactly she should or should not reveal. "Nope, not much. He was not from Jefferson County; I can tell you that. He dressed nicely and seemed to have a roll of dough in his pocket."

I decide to push further. "How did he treat Gracie?"

"She fell head over heels for that man, don't you know. Once she met Jefferson they spent plenty of time together. I only got to talk to him without Gracie around once or twice."

"Did you ever go with them to Beaver Falls?"

"How did you know about that?" she seems shocked.

"I stumbled onto some information in cleaning out some of Gracie's papers."

Charisse is silent for a minute. I can tell she is hesitating for a reason. "I was dating someone else at the time. I was busy. I may have gone with them once to Beaver Falls."

"Did you ever take a photo of Jefferson and Gracie together?"

"I didn't own a camera."

"How long did they date before getting married?"

"Seemed like only four months. Your father had a car and one weekend they left town and came back married. Gino and Viviana were not happy about it."

I realize Charisse is upset about this line of questions so I change the subject. I rattle off a couple of cute stories about the twins, and Charisse seems to relax. With our coffee cups refilled, we talk about Gracie's health and share how we both worry about her.

"I'll stop in at Silver Belles this afternoon," Charisse says.

I give her a big hug and hurry out.

CHAPTER 8

The leaves on the Steubenville trees are beginning to turn colors. I love this time of year. The weather is cooler, and I like taking walks in the park without getting overly sweaty. It's also the time when flowers look their best. The annuals in a well-tended garden swell to their peak of color as if to say, "We've done our best to make your life more pleasant, but soon we will be gone." Sure enough, a hard freeze will kill them overnight. The petunias, snapdragons, and impatiens will shrivel into a clump and tell the gardener that if they want more of the same next year, they must plant new cousins in the spring to take their place.

Cousins. If I have any, I'm not certain who they are. My Aunt Bee never married, and Grandpa Gino's cousin Sal never had children. Grandpa said that Sal died of disease, but I'm not certain that he wasn't shot in a robbery or some other kind of crime. I know nothing about the Bergstroms so it is possible I have some cousins on that side of my family, but I don't know. That's one of the things I'm trying to find out.

My favorite place to walk is the Beatty Park Trail. It's a 1.7-mile loop that's easy to negotiate, and I have the option to bring Silky. I especially love to walk here when I'm feeling tense. I love the fact the Dino Dash is held here every June during the Dean Martin Festival. Runners sign up for a 5K run/walk along the purple or red trails that make a short loop adjacent to Union Cemetery. They start at 8:00 a.m. so everyone can get to the Rat Pack Parade along Fourth Street, which starts at noon.

I spend an hour on the trail and feel both tired and invigorated at the same time. It's a great boost to my disposition, but it also leaves me famished. I plan to stop on the way home and pick up a strawberry milkshake. It reminds me that I need to take one to Gracie next time I go to see her.

• • •

I haven't checked my desktop computer since last night, so I sit down expecting the usual mix of spam and junk email that seems never ending. One email catches my eye right away. The genealogist I hired to search my family, Juliette Mirow, has sent me a report.

It seems Juliette has completed a preliminary search on the Bergstroms and has started the search on the Rivers family line. I print out everything she has sent and plop into my comfy chair. My heart races as I stare at the cover pages. *Will my father's identity be in here?*

Juliette has traced Jefferson Arno Bergstrom Jr. back to his grandfather Nils Bergstrom, born in Aroostook County, Maine. Jefferson's grandmother's name is Annika, born in Sweden.

Juliette reports that the Bergstrom trail from there will lead deep into Sweden, and she would like to pursue it, if I so desire. She will have a report soon on the Rivers family, but I already know that Gino's parents were from the Calabria region of Italy and Viviana was born there. Juliette says if I want to know more about the Bergstroms, there will be additional fees. She has a contact in Stockholm who can help. I tell her to pause the search for now so I can process the details on three known generations of Bergstroms—my paternal family.

Aroostook County, Maine, lies along the US–Canadian border (pop. 67,105) just west of the Canadian province of New Brunswick. Four Bergstroms were born there: Nils Bergstrom (1892), his son Jefferson (1915), and his twins, Erik and Astrid (1919). It appears that Jefferson A. Bergstrom Jr.—*my father*—was born in 1937 in North Creek, New York. His mother's name was Eleanora.

There it is—the birthplace I've been seeking. It only takes me a minute to connect North Creek with the nearby Barton Garnet Mines. Bingo! I see on a map that North Creek is in Warren County, New York. I pick up my iPad and use the search engine to see what cities are in the area. The resort town of Lake George is a few miles from there, and further south is Saratoga Springs. The latter has a casino. Perfect—Charisse loves casinos, and maybe I can talk her into a joy ride to upstate New York. I discover the distance between Steubenville and Saratoga Springs is eight hours by car. We can get there in a day's drive, stay a couple days, and drive back. I'll call Charisse later.

I look up the address of the office of the county clerk. The records room appears to be in the Warren County Municipal

Center on State Route 9 in Lake George. Here lies another clue—*Gracie had an ashtray from Lake George*. My plan is taking shape! Charisse could gamble in the casino in Saratoga Springs while I spend the day in Lake George. I cross my fingers and hope she buys it.

I turn my research to the Bergstroms from the state of Maine. A map shows some of the coastal towns have names I slightly recognize—Bar Harbor, Camden, Cape Elizabeth, Kennebunkport, and Portland.

Further research reveals there is a Swedish colony in northern Maine consisting of the towns of New Sweden, Stockholm, Woodland, Connor, Westerland, Madawaska Lake, and Caribou.

The state apparently began to recruit Scandinavian immigrants in the 1860s to establish a new agricultural settlement in the virgin forest area of Aroostook County. The first colonists arrived in 1870 and named their town New Sweden. Each family received a cabin and 100 acres of forest with five acres cleared.

As a history teacher, I can't wait to dig into this story. I'm tempted to drop everything and head to Maine, but I know I can't do that right now. I'm going to limit my travel plans to a possible trip to upstate New York. Now I've got to enlist Charisse.

• • •

I call Charisse and explain my plan, which includes a hotel stay at the Saratoga Springs casino and research in Lake George. I also add a possible run to the Barton Mines in North Creek. Charisse sounds intrigued and loves hearing about the genealogist's report. I ask her if she will travel with me.

"I'd love to go with you. If I move a doctor's appointment and cancel my haircut I can go the week after next," she says with enthusiasm.

"Great! I'll make the reservations—my treat."

"Oh no, honey," she argues. "I'll pay my share of the lodging."

"You can buy the first tank of gas for the trip. That's good enough. I need a sidekick."

• • •

Saturday comes, and Bridgette has a few free hours to herself. Joe decides to spend some 'dad time' with the twins by taking them to a movie, and Bridgette is up for a walk with me in Beatty Park.

We decide to take the stone steps, which always gives me a cardio workout. At age 62, I'm not a spring chicken. I'm gassed by the time we get to the top, and we decide to sit for a minute on a bench.

I take time to explain my plans for the trip to upstate New York. Bridgette is anxious for me to flush out any family information I can find. The Swedish connection both fascinates and animates us. We imagine having distant cousins in Maine.

"We might have to eat lutefisk," she laughs.

"Dried cod soaked in lye is not my idea of a delicacy. I don't know how the Swedes do it."

We both laugh and Bridgette switches topics.

"Are you going to tell Grandma Gracie that you are making a trip with Charisse?"

"I don't think so. She will probably say she wants to go along too, and we know that's impossible. I don't want to upset her."

"While you're gone, I'll go visit with her," Bridgette says. "I'll take Olivia. She has been asking about Gracie, and she wants to give her some drawings."

As we relax on the bench, relishing the sound of the birds gossiping in the trees, we realize there is a slight rustling. "I think the noise is getting louder," Bridgette says. "The birds are discussing their southern escape."

Escape. The word itself connotes both danger and excitement. I've lived my whole life in a town I should have permanently escaped when I came of age. I stayed because of Gracie, and when Gracie escapes her life on Earth maybe I'll escape Steubenville.

• • •

"Did you go to Mass today?" Gracie asks.

It's a Monday, and I never attended Mass on a Monday, even as a young parishioner 45 years ago. Gracie has forgotten that I dropped away and consider myself somewhere between a lapsed and a recovering Catholic. During my junior year of high school, I found myself numb every time I sat in the pews. I simply found no joy in the music, the homily, and the supposed majesty of it all. I felt entrapped while inside those walls.

Gracie was very disappointed, but she didn't harass me about it. She and Grandma Viviana continued to attend services each Sunday. They prayed to the Blessed Virgin for me to return to the church. I relented a little—I attended Midnight Mass on Christmas Eve with them each year, but that was it. When my grandmother died, Gracie went alone.

I married Anders when I was 21. He was a faithful Methodist and took Bridgette and Toby to Sunday school. I would attend Easter and Christmas services with them, but that's all. Any tiny ounce of church spirituality I felt was brittle. It got worse when Toby died. If I had felt empty before, it got worse after that. I threw my life into teaching history and enjoying music. I relished listening to Bridgette practicing her lessons—first piano and clarinet, then violin. I bought a better stereo system (with our store discount) and plenty of CDs. I became obsessed with jazz—something I never liked before Toby's death—but the music of Dizzy Gillespie and Miles Davis seemed to free me.

I suddenly snap away from my deep thoughts and fib to Gracie. "Yes, Mom. I went to Mass." I figure God will forgive me as I try to comfort my mother in some small way.

Anders was very patient with me. He spent a lot of time expanding his electronics store and making it a success. His side hustle of buying and selling antiques was also a distraction for him when he was home trying to decompress from a long day. I was lucky that he did not indulge in alcohol or other vices as others who have lost a child. He was a good man and did not deserve the health issues that overcame him in his 50s. Bridgette and I did what we could to make him feel needed and comfortable. Still, in all, it did not help me feel closer to my faith.

Not so for Bridgette. She attended Mass with Gracie and converted to Catholicism. I stayed home and listened to ballads by Barbra, Beyonce, Rihanna, and Adele. I cleaned my house to J.Lo and played classical music when I graded papers or wrote tests.

Music helped to soothe me. I felt that I didn't need to go to church on any kind of regular basis. The two times a year I sat in the pews I closed myself off and concentrated on history—history with a backdrop of pipe organ music. I imagined being with Bach, Mozart, and Beethoven from the Classical period, and Haydn and Schubert from the Baroque. I remembered that we were taught Antonio Vivaldi was a Catholic priest. Furthermore, Palestrina was known for a variety of sacred genres, including masses and madrigals. But most of all, he is known for music written for use in Catholic worship services.

All of this has disappeared from Gracie's memory bank. The spark plug that fires the synapses in her brain is now on the fritz. I don't see any way it's coming back. Each week Gracie gets a little weaker.

"Did you remember to turn off the teapot?" Gracie asks.

"Yes, I did."

"Where's my newspaper? I haven't seen it today."

"I'll bring it tomorrow." In truth, she hasn't asked for it in months and I cancelled her subscription.

"Make sure you bring my checkbook too," she demands. "I need a new car."

I slip out of Silver Belles and make my way to my 10-year-old Dodge Caravan—the last car Anders purchased before he died. I hope it runs for 10 more years.

CHAPTER 9

Charisse and I sit across from each other in the Saratoga Springs Resort, ready to order cocktails.

"I'll have a glass of Pinot Noir," I say to the server.

"Give me a shot of Jack Daniels, straight—no chaser," Charisse says with an experienced flair.

The server nods and disappears.

We begin to review our trip so far. Our eight-hour drive across Pennsylvania and New York went smoothly thanks to a stack of various musicals on CDs (*Evita, Phantom of the Opera, Grease*) I brought along in the car to entertain us on the boring turnpike drive. Charisse loved it.

We sip our drinks and reminisce about our first full day in Saratoga Springs. Charisse says she buzzed the casino and staked out a chair for a day-long pull on a slot machine. Meanwhile, I tell her how I drove to the Warren County Municipal Center to search for info on the Bergstroms.

"What did you find?" Charisse asks anxiously.

"It turns out my father was born in Warren County. His

mother's full name is Eleanora Birdsong. Can you believe it? Birdsong!"

"That sounds like a Native American name," Charisse replies.

"I think so too. I found an address for the library in North Creek. It's just a little town, and I'm sure it won't be hard to find. We'll start our search there. North Creek is right along the Hudson River in the mountains."

"I'm guessing there are lots of ski lodges up there. I had a cousin who went to Gore Mountain a couple times to ski. That's too cold for me. I'd rather sit in the lodge next to a fire and drink champagne," Charisse laughs.

"Do you want to ride with me tomorrow to check out the town? I could use a navigator."

"Sure. I've spent my wad of money anyhow."

"Let's leave right after breakfast."

• • •

We head north into the Adirondack Mountains to search the village of North Creek. As we drive along, there are signs everywhere for scenic trails, waterfalls, shops, and restaurants. We pull over at a scenic overlook and fill our souls with nature's beauty. The majesty of the mountains makes me feel both diminished and heightened. Suddenly a hawk flies overhead looking for a tasty critter on which to dine. In the distance birds chatter. Wisps of cool air float overhead. The sun glistens off the mountainside. I'm tingling with excitement.

Not only does this area look like a gorgeous place to ski but also to fish and camp. Anders would have loved it and, for a few minutes, I feel the overwhelming pangs of missing him as well as Toby.

Anders had taken Toby fishing four times before "The Accident." It was an excellent experience for them both. Their fishing poles now sit side by side in my basement, along with their hats and Anders's tackle box. It's my own personal shrine to their memory.

We get back in the car, and soon we're in the village of North Creek. The first stop is to visit the Johnsburg Public Library for more research. After that I plan to take us to the Barton Mines for a tour. Charisse and I walk into the library armed with stenographer's notebooks and pens. A board of notices greets us with the week's events—Trivia Night, Lego Club, Story Hour, and Table Plays. As I research old locations for the local post office, town hall, and schools, Charisse digs through 1940s phone books. She also volunteers to look through school yearbooks for Jefferson's photo since she knows what he looks like. After two hours we meet in the adult fiction section.

"I've got two addresses for Bergstroms," Charisse says almost breathlessly. "One from 1940 and one from 1945."

"Terrific. We'll try to find those houses. There is only one school building in town, and it's a central school. All classes pre-K to high school go there. I also have the old address for the town hall."

"One more thing, Mo," Charisse says timidly. "I found a picture of your father in a high school yearbook. Come, I'll show you."

My knees start to buckle. An actual picture! Am I finally going to see an image of the most mysterious person in my life?

Charisse grabs the yearbook and turns to a page showing 15 children in three rows—the entire freshmen class of Johnsburg High School in 1952. Though the image is small, I can see a family resemblance. I hug the book to my chest and ask an information associate if I can make two copies of the page on the library's photocopy machine. It takes only a minute (and 40 cents in fees), and we head back to the car. I am practically in a daze.

"What does it feel like to see him?" Charisse asks.

"My emotions are a mix between elation and sorrow," I reply. "But I'm thrilled with what we have found."

We see the central school building on Main Street ("Home of the Jaguars") and speculate that my father would have attended there from first through ninth grade. After that, it's another mystery. Charisse could not find a photo of him in any yearbook past freshman year.

We find where the old post office had once been located. It is now a barber shop, and I wonder how many times my father's parents and even my father had been in that building. We stop and I take a photo with my iPhone camera.

Next we drive to an address Charisse found for my grandparents' home in 1940. It is a little Cape Cod that reminds me of Gracie's house in Mingo Junction but in much worse shape. The roof needs replacing and the house could use a new coat of paint. I take a photo there too.

Finally, we drive to the address for my grandparents' home in 1945. The address is on Main Street, and the structure is now a two-story law office. The building looks well maintained and has a parking lot. I pull in.

"This is brave of you," Charisse says.

"I need an excuse to go inside," I say, my brain in overdrive. I think for a minute and say to Charisse, "I've got it. Be right back."

I bravely walk the trim brick sidewalk to the front and see a sign on the office door: *Vermeyen & Vermeyen—Attorneys-at-Law*. Before I chicken out, I spring inside and spot a friendly-looking receptionist talking on the phone. I'm in no rush for her to finish her conversation—*my father once lived here*! I tap my foot nervously but it gives me a minute to look around. Soon enough she hangs up and asks how she can help me.

"I'm from out of town," I stammer, "but I may have some legal work I need done here. I'm looking for an attorney."

"What kind of legal help do you need?"

Damn it. What do I say? "Real estate. I want to buy property here."

"Yes, we handle that at our firm," she replies. "Take one of our cards. You can call for an appointment."

I gladly take one fast look around and see there is a hallway that goes towards the back of the house. How many times did my father and my grandparents walk through here? I start to feel shaky and spot a nearby water cooler sitting under a painting depicting the village.

"May I take a drink? My throat's dry."

"Sure, help yourself."

"That's a lovely painting."

"Yes, my grandfather painted it in 1960. The village hasn't changed much since then. He went on to become the mayor in the 1970s."

"By the way, my friend and I are looking for a good place for a late lunch. Any suggestions?"

"If you like Alpine food, Beck's Tavern is very popular."
"Perfect!"

• • •

Charisse and I are sitting in the tavern looking at the menu. The German dishes all look scrumptious. I can't decide whether I want sauerbraten or pork schnitzel. Charisse, whose father was a Swiss chef, was drawn to either the Weisswurst or the spaetzle with beef tips. We both agree that we will pass on the poutine—a Canadian specialty dish made with cheese curds.

"Whatever we order, we must share an appetizer of sauerkraut balls," she says.

As we each slurp down a glass of Chardonnay, we plan our next move.

"You know, Charisse, we're going to have to come back to this town."

"I agree. For one thing, it's beautiful. For another, I can see you are drawn to this place. If you need a companion for another trip, I'm game."

"It's a deal! We'll be better prepared next time."

• • •

The trip from downtown North Creek to the Barton Mines above the hamlet of North River (pop. 144) takes about ten minutes. The luscious green mountains are beginning to crown with the golden glow of fall. We pull into the parking lot not knowing what to expect on this leg of our adventure.

We head into the gift shop to pay the entrance fee. A big sign proudly tells us that garnets are the state gem of New York. I had checked a trip advisor website before we left Ohio, and it advised us to bring along plastic zip bags, scoops, gloves, and strainers for collecting garnets.

We buy our tickets and head out to the tour's mine site. The path is a magic carpet of tiny gem fragments sparkling in the afternoon sun. These fragments are left when the garnets are harvested and ground for use as abrasives. All along our path people are huddled next to two ponds, sifting for gems. Children giggle and adults grin as they find tiny red gems among the silt and sand.

Charisse and I soon join the collectors with our scoops and gloves, and before long, we have each gathered about half a small sandwich bag of glittery rocks.

Back at the gift shop, our two baggies are weighed, and we are charged 30 cents each to take home our loot.

"I've never had so much fun for under a dollar," Charisse says.

"Yes," I reply. "I'd say it is a great way to end our first adventure to upstate New York. I'll be sad to leave. I feel like I've really bonded with the area."

• • •

Charisse and I are driving the Pennsylvania Turnpike heading back to Steubenville. We've had a successful trip but there are plenty of questions left unanswered.

"We now know that my father attended school in North Creek, so that's a good start. The second home he lived in seems quite nice, so his father must have had a good job. What next?"

"It's possible that the family moved or that your father dropped out of school," Charisse says. "Do you suppose he enlisted in the military?"

"That's a good question. I'm hoping the genealogist can track that down for me."

"Maybe you can access the local newspaper archives like you did in Beaver Falls. Try Saratoga Springs, then Lake George, and even little North Creek. It's amazing the info people can access online."

"When I get home I'm going to search the Find a Grave site. I meant to do that before we left on the trip."

"I know it is important to you to try and find a genetic link to the Bergstroms to help the doctors treat Max," Charisse says. "He's such a great kid and he deserves a healthy life."

"Did I tell you I've contacted a DNA testing company to try and find relatives?"

Charisse sucks in her breath, and I can see she is surprised. "No, you didn't tell me. That's a great idea."

I can tell that Charisse is mulling something over in her mind. Whatever she's thinking, she's not telling me.

The nine-hour drive comes to an end, and I drop Charisse off at her condo. She gives me a hug and scoots off. "You did a great job, Mo," she says. "With your determination, you'll find what you're looking for."

I reach my own home and realize I am too tired to eat dinner. I text Bridgette to confirm I am back and thank her for watching the dog. I feed Silky and glance quickly at the mail. It can wait until tomorrow.

I tumble into bed, and Silky snuggles beside me. She has missed me. Normally I fall right asleep, but now I just toss and turn. I get up and go to the desktop. I enter *Jefferson A. Bergstrom, Sr.* into the Find a Grave search engine. It takes a minute and then—bam! Date of birth—2/15/1915. Date of death—3/30/62. Burial site—Glens Falls Cemetery, Glens Falls, New York. He was 47 years old. One question rises to the top: Why so young?

I've now become obsessed with finding more. I research names of newspapers around North Creek and Warren County, New York. Once I uncover newspaper archival sites, I search the obituaries. By 3:00 a.m. I find the man who is my grandfather.

> *Jefferson A. Bergstrom, Sr., Glen Falls, formerly of North Creek. Former manager at Barton Mines in North Creek. Member of American Legion Post 629. Predeceased by parents Nils & Annika Bergstrom and son Jefferson Bergstrom, Jr. Survived by wife Eleanora, daughter Elin, brother Erik of Maine, & sister Astrid of Glens Falls, nieces and nephews.*

I feel totally spent. It's now 4:00 a.m. and I have many errands to run tomorrow. I head back to bed where Silky is sleeping with her head on my pillow. I don't have the energy to move her so I get another pillow and crash onto the mattress. I'll sleep better knowing I'm on the right track.

CHAPTER 10

I'm feeling chipper after my trip to upstate New York with Charisse. I have clues to help dig into my Bergstrom family. I still have the feeling Charisse knows more than she is telling me, but I'll deal with that later.

I park my Caravan in the Silver Belles lot and head inside carrying yellow mums in a pot. Fall is the perfect season for mums in Ohio. I enter Gracie's room and come to a dead stop. Sitting next to Gracie's bed are two police officers I do not recognize. Both look like salesmen for Barstools-R-Us.

"Hello, Mrs. Albrecht. We thought we'd drop by to talk to your mother," one says casually.

"I can see that," I reply tartly.

"She told us her father was a nice man who took very good care of her and her mother, Viviana."

I start to panic. "What else has she told you?" I blurt out sharply.

"She said she loves the drawings your granddaughter made her," one replies, pointing to two of Olivia's newest creations. "We've just wrapped things up so we'll be on our way."

They leave, and I spend the next five minutes pacing the room, pretending I am straightening Gracie's clothes. I'm waiting to make certain the policemen aren't coming back. It's time to quiz down Gracie.

"What did those two men ask you?"

"They wanted to know where they could buy some cigars."

I do a slow burn, realizing they were pumping her for info on Grandpa Gino.

"What else did they ask?"

"I don't remember," Gracie sighs.

"Did they ask about the baubles?" I say, remembering she had used that term with me two months ago.

"Yes," Gracie says with a slight smile.

I realize the police are still digging around for info connected to the garnets and God knows what else.

"Can you remember any other questions they asked?"

"Those men wanted to know about the red ponies," Gracie says flatly.

"Huh? What are red ponies?"

"You know."

"I honestly don't, Mom."

"Go see your grandfather. He'll tell you."

Bridgette and I are in her kitchen making several pans of lasagna for an orchestra fundraising dinner. After the pans are assembled, Joe will pack them in his SUV and deliver them to the school kitchen where they'll be baked. It gives me a chance to give Bridgette details of my trip to upstate New York.

"So, you were inside the house where Jefferson and his parents lived? That's astounding!" Bridgette declares.

"I was so nervous I could hardly speak," I admit.

"Did you get any new information out of Charisse? Did anything trigger a memory from her short time knowing him? I mean, she found his picture in a school yearbook."

"It's odd, isn't it? She says she saw him infrequently in the brief time he lived in Steubenville, and I believe her. But she and Gracie have always been very close—as close as twins. I have a feeling she knows more."

"What else did you find?"

"At the county municipal center, I found Jefferson's mother's full name. It's Eleanora Birdsong. Amazing, huh? She's my paternal grandmother."

"Birdsong! That sounds like a Native American name."

"Charisse and I think so too. I also went online late last night and found an obituary for my grandfather in a New York newspaper. I'll bring it over next time and we'll go through it—maybe even start a chart so we can follow our new relatives."

• • •

I'm headed to the Steubenville Post Office to mail back my completed DNA kit. I'm feeling nervous. I've read articles in various publications on how these DNA tests can open doors to people connecting with unknown relatives. Most stories are positive, but a few have turned out badly. Still, I won't know until I've tried. Nothing ventured, nothing gained.

On the drive to the post office, I steer past the site of Viviana's old store—Passages. I think about my grade-school friends who had birthday parties where both of their grandmothers attended.

I only had one grandmother—yet she was kind and supportive. Imagine if I had had two—Viviana Rivers and Eleanora Birdsong Bergstrom? Would they have gotten along? So many questions fill my brain.

Viviana Marie Tattini Rivers was born in Italy in 1915— the daughter of Italians living in Naples. Her father, Arturo, had grown up around the docks in the port city and picked up small labor jobs as a teenager rather than going to school. He and Viviana's mother, Rosa, married at age 17 and had their daughter a year later. They wanted a better life for the family so they found passage to New York where an uncle was living. Once in America, the uncle suggested he join his cousin running boats down the Ohio River to Wheeling. The job on the river did not suit Arturo's taste and soon he took a job with the Wheeling Steel Corporation in Wheeling, West Virginia. A couple years later he transferred to their plant in Mingo Junction.

I never knew Arturo or Rosa. They both died before I was born. But Viviana spoke well of them. Once, when Viviana was driving me past the site of the Mingo Junction steel plant, she told me her father was always proud that George Washington once camped on the barren ground along the river in October of 1770. He, his friend Colonel William Crawford, and a few other men were surveying land along the Ohio River and camped there among the Iroquois.

• • •

I'm sitting in my comfy armchair watching the 1959 Western *Rio Bravo* with Dean Martin playing a drunk named Dude. The cast includes John Wayne, Angie Dickinson, and Ricky Nelson. The plot revolves around a sheriff (Wayne) who must hold a murder suspect (Claude Akins) until a US Marshal arrives. I love watching Angie play a prostitute and Ricky, a real teenage heartthrob in those days, play a gunslinger. It's Hollywood at its cheesiest, and I wonder if my parents went to see the movie together since it was released in 1959—the year they married.

At the conclusion of the movie, I discover the Library of Congress selected this film in 2014 for preservation in the National Film Registry. I wonder if Steubenville's native son has any other movies in the prestigious archives.

• • •

Two events have interrupted my normally docile life this week. Both are family medical issues. First, Bridgette broke her ankle playing outside with her dog. She must undergo surgery in Steubenville on Friday, and Joe will be with her.

The second problem gives me greater concern. Max has not been well and needs some special medical tests that can't be done locally. These tests can be performed at either Children's Hospital of Pittsburgh or Wheeling Children's Hospital. Bridgette and Joe opt for Pittsburgh, and Max's tests are scheduled for Friday also. They asked if I would take him, and I readily agree. We must leave at 7:00 a.m. I ask Charisse if she will go along with me as navigator. She agrees.

• • •

I've rarely been to Pittsburgh, but I like it here. It's a beautiful fall day, sunny but cool—what we call "jacket weather." Joe and Max are big Steelers football fans, and today Max has proudly worn his black and gold shirt. There is a big game this weekend, and many of the people in the hallways of the hospital are wearing Steelers apparel. Max is all smiles seeing so many people in his favorite colors. I'm glad he seems relaxed.

We arrive at the Pediatric Endocrinology Clinic and sign in. I promise Max that once he is finished, I will take him to the hospital cafeteria and he can pick out anything he wants to eat, including his favorite ice cream sundae. He's all smiles. Two women in colorful lab coats come out to retrieve him and explain that it will take over an hour for the testing. They assure Max that everything will be fine and that they will bring him back to grandma as soon as possible. He nods.

• • •

Our tummies are full as we head towards home. Max says he's feeling well so I ask him if he and Charisse would like to see some history at the Fort Pitt Museum and the Heinz History Center at Point State Park. The spot is located at the confluence of the Monongahela and Allegheny Rivers, which forms the Ohio River. I would love to make this an impromptu field trip in history *and* geography. Both agree and we're on our way. I laugh to myself, thinking that since I'm a history teacher, my grandson would not dare to defy me and say he doesn't want to go. He smiles in approval.

We step inside the Fort Pitt Museum and soak in the sights of the exhibits. I explain about Guyasuta, a Seneca chief, who became the premiere leader of the Iroquois Confederacy in the Ohio Valley.

There are replicas of both Fort Pitt and Fort Duquesne on display. The latter was built by the French in 1754 during the French and Indian War. At the Battle of Fort Duquesne in 1758, the French defeated the British, but French officers knew they would soon be overtaken by the forces of General John Forbes. They ordered the fort to be destroyed and abandoned. The British then built Fort Pitt at the Point near the same site. The Fort Pitt Blockhouse still survives. It is believed to be the oldest building still standing in Pittsburgh.

By the end of two hours, I can see that both Max and Charisse are tired and it is time to head home. We take the Fort Pitt Bridge over the Monongahela River and into the Fort Pitt Tunnel through the South Shore neighborhood. Max is impressed with the bridge and tunnel. "Awesome! That was fun." But 15 minutes later he is asleep in the back of the car, so it is a good time to talk to Charisse.

"If it turns out that Eleanora Birdsong Bergstrom is a Native American, I'm going to make a day trip back here to dig inside the Heinz Historical Center's archives. It appears that they have all kinds of great genealogical information. We're lucky to have something like that close to home."

"I absolutely agree," Charisse replies. "This has been my first trip to the Point. All my other trips here involved Pirates games or the Rivers Casino."

"You know, I didn't expect my retirement to have so much drama. Once Mom got sick I really started digging into my family's history. It's a strange mix of Italians, Swedes, and possibly even Native Americans. Between the genealogist and the DNA testing, there are still more things to come. I'm both excited and apprehensive."

Charisse is quiet for a moment, and I can see she is thinking about what to say. "Just remember, Mo, that some things might not be as they seem and some things might be more than they seem. Life is full of twists and turns. I hope, for your sake, it's a good experience."

CHAPTER 11

I'm driving past the local high school, and I see a sign board advertising the drama department's fall play *Chicago*. I loved being involved in drama during high school. We performed *The Diary of Anne Frank* and *Camelot,* among other plays, but the musicals were my favorite. One of my girlfriends played Guinevere in *Camelot,* and I played Lady Catherine. It was the most fun—a huge cast and lots of high energy.

At the stop light I catch myself singing "The Simple Joys of Maidenhood" out loud in the car. By the time I get to the grocery store I've sung "I Wonder What the King is Doing Tonight." While wheeling my cart down the aisle searching for Olivia's favorite pretzels, I'm humming "What Do the Simple Folks Do?" I hope I don't see anyone I know. I grab the pretzels and my favorite breakfast cereal (which sometimes serves as my dinner) and head home.

I pull into my garage and spot Anders's favorite baseball hat hanging from a bare nail. I think about how Anders drove me back and forth to college several times before he asked me out.

Then I think about *Camelot* and the song "I loved You Once in Silence." I tell myself not to think about him right now. It's too sad. I put my groceries away and get ready to prepare rotini and meatballs for myself. I realize the lights and stove in the kitchen don't work, so the circuit breaker must have popped. I go to the sink and find there is a constant drip coming out. It's annoying. I don't know how to fix these things so I'll ask my son-in-law Joe to come tomorrow. I grab a bowl and pour myself some cereal. What kind of wine goes with Cocoa Puffs? *Sigh*—the life of a widow.

The electricity is still working in the house so I go into the basement to run some laundry. A few feet from the washer is a box marked *books* that had been in Gracie's house. I forgot I had asked Bridgette to carry it down here a couple months ago.

The box holds a variety of literary favorites—classics like *A Tree Grows in Brooklyn* by Betty Smith, autobiographies like *The Lonely Life* by Bette Davis, and cookbooks like *Mastering the Art of French Cooking* by Julia Child.

At the bottom of the box, I find a surprise—*A Coney Island of the Mind* by Lawrence Ferlinghetti. I grab *Coney Island* and head upstairs to my armchair. Gracie always told me never to scribble inside a book because it ruins the pages. But inside are notes in the margins or stars drawn next to certain lines. I thumb through poem after poem searching for something familiar—something I have seen in a note she secreted away. It doesn't take long to find it. It's the beginning of Chapter 8.

The world is a beautiful place
  to be born into

> *if you don't mind happiness*
>   *not always being*
>   *so very much fun*
> *if you don't mind a touch of hell*
>   *now and then*
> *just when everything is fine*
>   *because even in heaven*
>   *they don't sing*
>   *all the time*

There it is! The poem found in Gracie's desk—the one where someone had copied it from Ferlinghetti's book and signed it "C." Was it Charisse's lamentations, or was it, dare I think, Carlton's?

• • •

Gracie is fumbling with a piece of paper and a pencil as I enter her room.

"I'm making a shopping list. I need five pounds of bologna and buns."

"For God's sake, why?"

"People are coming in and out all day to visit me. They need to eat. They need hospitality."

"I'm not doing that."

She ignores me. "Mustard too. Do you still make rye toast with a piece of cheese on top for breakfast?" Gracie asks.

I've never done that but I don't want to upset her. "Yes, I do."

"I want rye toast. And Raisin Bran. And a banana."

"I'll tell the staff."

"One more thing," Gracie says with a concerned look. "Your grandmother is very worried."

"She can't be worried, Mom," I say. "She's been dead for 23 years."

"No, she's not. I just saw her and she said she is worried about the red ponies."

Once again she is talking about red ponies, and I have no idea what she is trying to tell me. I head out to leave Silver Belles and run into a fellow retired teacher from my school. We decide to sit in the lobby for a few minutes to compare notes on retirement. When she gets up to go visit her father, I spy a regional magazine sitting on the coffee table in front of me dated from July. The cover has a full-page photo of James Traficant—a notorious former Congressman from eastern Ohio. The title above his image says *Youngstown's Most Famous Crook,* with the subhead blaring, *Traficant - The Life & Legend of a Native Son.*

I pick up the magazine and read the article marking the twentieth anniversary of his death. I remember that Grandpa Gino told me that he met him once and found him exceedingly arrogant.

"He could piss off the Pope," grandpa said at the time.

Hard-luck Youngstown, once a booming steel town, is just an hour's drive north of Steubenville. It was once caught between the Cleveland and Pittsburgh mob factions. For many years Cleveland's mobsters had more dominance, but during the 1970s, a full-blown war raged among factions in Cleveland. The most famous of these battles occurred in the mid to late 1970s between mob bosses James "Blackie" Licavoli and Irish Danny Greene. It took a major toll on the Lake Erie mob.

Meanwhile, there were plenty of illegal businesses to control in Youngstown. It legitimately earned the nickname "Crimetown." In 1980, James Traficant was elected sheriff of Mahoning County, where Youngstown is located. Before he had served his first day as sheriff, Traficant held a meeting with Cleveland mobsters to chat about $163,000 in illegal cash given by both Cleveland and Pittsburgh hoodlums to run his campaign. Little did he know that one of the men had taped the conversation with the flamboyant Mr. T declaring he would use his law enforcement superpowers to take on the Pittsburgh mob.

In 1983, the FBI took him to trial, where he was accused of accepting bribes from the mob while serving as sheriff. Traficant, who acted as his own attorney (without a law degree), razzle-dazzled the jury and preyed on their suspicions about the federal government. He was acquitted, becoming the only person to win a RICO case while representing himself.

Traficant then ran for Congress in 1984 and won—taking his talents to Washington, D.C., where his message of economic populism played well with his constituents. Alas, his luck ran out.

In 2001, Traficant was back in federal court, charged with taking campaign funds for personal use. Once again, he represented himself. This time, however, he was convicted of ten felony counts, including bribery, racketeering and tax evasion. On July 24, 2002, he was expelled from the US House of Representatives.

I walk out to my car trying to tie things together. There has been so much history of mob crime in Steubenville, Cleveland, Youngstown, and Pittsburgh. So many secrets, so many hidden doors. I wish I could ask Gracie some specific questions. It doesn't help that she makes screwball comments about red ponies. What if red ponies have an actual meaning other than the color of horse flesh?

I'm suddenly struck with a question. Is there a criminal connection to the phrase? Who would know? I have just the right person. I pull out my iPhone and find myself calling Tim Konig. He answers almost immediately.

"Hi, Mrs. Albrecht," he says brightly. "I'm surprised to hear from you."

"Tim, I want to avoid any connection to your fellow officers, but I have a question. Can I count on you not to discuss this conversation with anyone?"

"Sure. What's up?"

"Are the words 'red pony' code for something illegal?"

There is silence on his end for a few seconds. Then he clears his throat. "Well, yes. The Cosa Nostra used it as code around here for their fencing operations."

"Could you give me an example?" I ask.

"Okay, let's say someone was looking to make some illegal cash, so an individual knowingly buys stolen property and then resells it for a profit."

"Oh," I gulp. "Thanks, Tim."

"Let me know if you need anything else, Mrs. A," he says and hangs up.

Jesus, Mary, and Joseph, I think to myself, using one of Viviana's lamentations. What do I do now?

CHAPTER 12

The October breezes are fickle in Steubenville this time of year. Some days the breeze is light with edges of warmth. Other days it is loaded with a cold harsh warning that fall is in full tilt and edging toward winter.

I stand at my front window and watch the school kids on the street walking to their bus stop. Most of the boys still wear shorts, but the girls are dressed warmer. All are wearing jackets—girls with theirs zipped up, boys with theirs flapping open. I'm always amazed at how many boys don't wear socks. My feet are always cold so this is something I will never understand.

Watching children walk to school causes a knot to grow in my stomach. I would always take my two kids to the bus stop and make sure they got safely inside the vehicle. I was always so careful with them. Why did I let Toby ride his bike to the ball field that fateful day? Why didn't I drive him those three blocks and tell him to walk back to his grandmother's house? He begged me to let him ride that bike just like the other boys. I will never forgive myself.

A moody blue fog follows me as I go to my desktop computer to check for emails. One is from Juliette, the genealogist, who has some new information for me. Maybe this will brighten my disposition.

Juliette has found more of Gracie's Italian cousins who came to America. A couple of the relatives I already knew. Of more interest is some information on Eleanora Birdsong Bergstrom, my paternal grandmother. Eleanora's maternal grandmother was a member of the Seneca tribe. *Bingo!* Maybe that is the link to the postcard Gracie kept of Chief Cornplanter, whose uncle was Chief Guyasuta.

I feel very proud that I have a bit of Seneca ancestry—even though it goes back four or five generations. I'm now more determined to return to Pittsburgh's Heinz Historical Center to do research. Bridgette will also be excited about this new fact and will probably want to go with me.

The second piece of information is even more important to me. Juliette has found where my father joined the US Army at age 17 and served for three years. He was mustered out in Philadelphia. The only other piece of information she could find is that he and my mother were married in Pittsburgh in June of 1959. Did my mother suspect she was pregnant at the time?

My head is spinning. I'm suddenly rocked out of my blue mood, completely motivated to start digging into this new information.

I will follow up on my Seneca ancestry after I start investigating this new insight into my parents. I have so many questions. 1) What did Jefferson do in the army? 2) Where did he go after he was mustered out? 3) Where did Gracie meet Jefferson?

4) Why did Gracie run away from home to get married? 5) Why Pittsburgh? There is a pattern here, and I'm going to find where it leads. Jefferson's path somehow goes across Pennsylvania from Philly eventually to Steubenville over a six- or seven-year period. At some point before they were married, Gracie went to Beaver Falls. Is that where they met? And what was Jefferson doing in Beaver Falls?

I decide I must trace Jefferson's path from North Creek to Glens Falls and into the army. That's a good place to start. I also now have two reasons for another trip or two to Pittsburgh. One is to try and trace Eleanora and the other is to find my parents' marriage certificate at the Allegheny County Courthouse. Wait until I tell Bridgette!

I review the notes I took on my recent trip to North Creek. My father lived there from his birth in 1937 until at least 1952 or maybe 1954. If he had lived, he would be 85 years old now. Certainly, there are people who live in North Creek who would be around his age who possibly knew him. How can I contact people there without returning to the town?

I pull out the card of the receptionist from the attorney's office I visited. She told me her grandfather was once North Creek's mayor. How should I approach her? My mind is clicking. I jot down notes. Now all I need to do is work up some courage.

I am staring awkwardly at the painting of the yellow rooster I made for Gracie in fifth grade. I brought it home from her house last week because I just can't make myself throw it away. The rooster has crooked navy streaks running along the wings. Why? I don't remember.

It's silly that I can't make myself put this ugly thing in the trash—but I can't. To see something that Gracie loved for so many years literally kicked to the curb is too much for me right now. That stupid yellow rooster, that symbol of my younger self, is staring back and mocking me. Is that fair?

I am preparing myself to call the office administrator for the lawyer in North Creek. How should I sound? Anxious? Confident? Friendly? Professional? I don't have any expertise in real estate. I'm a retired history teacher. I'm also not good at lying—I'm too honest. I'm going to pretend I'm looking for real estate when, in fact, I'm really searching for information about my father. I'll never bring him back to earth but maybe I can touch the sky.

I dial the number while telling myself to stay calm.

"Vermeyen Law Office," the voice in North Creek says. "This is Greta. How can I help you?"

I explain that I had recently stopped by her office while looking to invest in real estate.

"My grandparents once lived in your town," I explain. "My father and his sister were raised there. I really like your area. It's beautiful."

"Why, thank you," Greta says. "We like it too. Not everyone can take the cold winters here. It helps if you are born into it or have connections. Otherwise, you want to live your winters in Florida like snowbirds."

I laugh slightly to match her cheery manner. But now I need to hone in on the real reason for my call.

"Greta, you told me when I was in your office that your grandfather was once mayor there. Is that correct?"

"Yes, he was," she says, "for eight years."

"Any chance he is still alive? I'm wondering if he knew my grandfather. The last name is Bergstrom—Jefferson Bergstrom Sr. He was a manager at Barton Mines."

"Ah yes, the mines. Most people who work there live in North Creek. When did he live here?"

"From the mid-1930s to the mid-1950s," I say. "I realize that's a long time ago, but I want to reconnect to the area."

"I see," Greta says wistfully. "Gore Mountain has that effect on some people. Unfortunately, my father died two years ago, but my aunt was a long-time clerk at the Johnsburg town hall. She's in her mid-80s but her mind is good. I can ask her."

"That would be so kind," I reply. "I'll give you my number. Please tell her to call anytime."

I hang up and realize my thumb and forefinger are numb from gripping the phone too tight. Was I that tense? I realize I never asked Greta about real estate transactions. She now has my phone number, which is good, but to keep up this ruse I better sound like I want to buy property. Joe has a cousin who sells real estate. I'll call her next.

• • •

Bridgette invites me to dinner after I call Joe. I never pass up an opportunity to see the twins, and I try to bring them something they will like. I spend an hour baking their favorite cookies while Silky runs in my fenced-in backyard. She chases a rabbit and two squirrels until it is time for me to leave.

Bridgette's house is abuzz with excitement. Joe and Max are cleaning out the RV and preparing it for winter. Max yells to me that he wants to talk about airplanes when he's done helping his dad. Olivia is anxious for me to see her new drawings. She is now into drawing animals and insects.

Bridgette asks about my phone conversation with the Vermeyen law office, and I tell them I need to sound like I'm serious about buying property. Joe asks why I don't just call the town hall myself and ask questions.

"Well, for one, my contact is in the law office that once was my grandfather's house, and I enjoy the vibe. I also have a hunch Greta may turn out to be helpful. If she doesn't come through, I'll call town hall myself."

"Make sure you have a price point in mind if you are going to talk about real estate," Joe says. "You might also do a Google Earth search of North Creek and surrounding Johnsburg Township so you can act like you've surveyed the area with real interest. I'm always shocked at what you can find about a geographic area without ever being there."

"Great idea," I reply. "I'll do it as soon as I go home."

• • •

I get home about 9:00 p.m. and decide to watch whatever film is on Turner Classic Movies. *Key Largo*, with Humphrey Bogart and Lauren Bacall, is about to start. It's one of my favorites. I make a big bowl of popcorn and start to relax. Naturally, the phone rings, and I see by caller ID that it is a New York area code.

"Is this Maureen Albrecht?" an elderly voice asks me.

"Yes, it is," I say as I mute the sound on the movie.

"My niece Greta Vermeyen gave me your phone number. My name is Bess Whitaker. Greta said your grandfather lived in North Creek."

"Yes, he and my grandmother lived there from the 1930s until the mid-1950s."

"I did meet your grandfather a couple times. He used to come into the town hall to get a hunting license. He had a teenage boy with him once."

"That would have been my father."

"Certainly. My memory is a little fuzzy these days. I started working at town hall during high school so it's obviously been a long time ago. I think the boy was tall and thin. I believe he had a paper route around town, but then the family moved."

"Do you happen to know why?"

"Hmmmm. I seem to remember that someone said Mr. Bergstrom was quite ill and was moving close to his family in Glens Falls. That's all I can remember."

"You've been most helpful, Ms. Whitaker. If you think of anything else, please call me. Thank you so much."

I'm dumbstruck—I've just talked to someone who once met my grandfather. I stare at the TV as I see Bogart light a cigarette. I remember a line I learned from reading movie history that Bogie used to say: "The whole world is three drinks behind. If everyone in the world takes three drinks, we would have no trouble."

I reach inside a cabinet where Anders kept his favorite drink—Old Grand-Dad bourbon. I pick up the bottle, hold it for a second, and set it back on the shelf. It's a nice memory thinking about how Anders enjoyed a nip now and then. It always relaxed him. He liked Bogart too. Occasionally he'd say, "Here's looking at you, kid," just like Bogie in *Casablanca*. If only he could be looking at me now.

CHAPTER 13

My conversation with Bess in North Creek confirms my suspicion that my grandfather must have moved to Glens Falls to be near family members as his health failed. It's not going to be easy to find a connection.

I am working at my desktop when a new email notice pops up on my screen. It's from the DNA testing company. I get a chill as I scramble to see what I hope is a treasure chest of family information. I'm not disappointed.

Before my eyes is a graphic that shows my test reveals I have the following lineage: 35% Scandinavian, 35% Italian, 10% Native American, 10% English/Scottish, and 10% Eastern European. More importantly, it lists the names of relatives who, likewise, put their DNA into the pool. There are several listed who can be traced to Gino and Viviana, which I expected. The others are from the Bergstrom side of my family. There is one of a woman in Pennsylvania. Here is my chance to connect. Do I have the guts to pursue it?

The woman's name is Ginger Keene. Pennsylvania has 13 million people, so finding her will be like searching for a needle in a haystack. I'll put her on hold while I go back and start combing through names from Glens Falls. The town's population is 14,784, so I have a better shot of finding a Bergstrom connection. Astrid may have gotten married and changed her last name. I also need to find my father's sister Elin. *She is my aunt—someone I didn't even know existed.* Is she still alive? If she is, that would give me a lot more information. My quest would be almost over.

A web search of Glens Falls reveals the Hudson River flows through the town and there are three unique waterfalls in the area. There are museums, festivals, theatre, concerts, and recreational activities. One eatery catches my eye—a place called Poopies Diner. How quaint! According to their web site, Poopies was started in 1954 by Joseph DiManno, the son of Italian immigrants. Joe's mother called him "Papino," a term of affection in Italian. The folks in the east end of Glens Falls started calling the diner "Poopies." They don't serve dinner—only breakfast and lunch. All sandwiches are served on grilled hard rolls, including the "Poopie burger." Gino and Viviana would approve.

I notice the diner opened in 1954. It's possible the Bergstroms ate there. I make notes on the place and will go there on my next trip to Warren County, New York. Maybe I can go again in late spring when there's no chance of snow. I don't want to drive on snowy roads in a strange environment.

I know that my grandparents and their daughter, Elin, left North Creek in the mid-1950s, so there must be some trace of them in Glens Falls. If Elin got married in town, there must be a record. I know Astrid lived there too. Did she ever get married? Did Elin finish high school there? I don't even know Elin's age. I only know she is younger than my father. So many questions.

I do a computer search and find one newspaper that was published from 1909–1971 (the *Post-Star*) and one that published from 1922–1971 (*Times*). A third newspaper, the *Chronicle*, has been published since 1980. If I search for a couple hours I may make a great discovery. Just then my cell phone rings and I see that someone from Silver Belles is calling.

"Mrs. Albrecht?"

"Yes."

"I'm calling from your mother's room. I'm Carin, her aide. Mrs. Rivers tumbled out of bed about an hour ago and scraped up her shin and knee. She's okay. The nurse has attended to the wounds. If you stop over today, Gloria, the head nurse, will go over everything. Mrs. Rivers has been given some medicine. She's asleep right now."

"I'll be over soon," I say. "Thanks."

I finish dressing, thankful that I am retired and can come and go as I please. All this would be much harder if I were still teaching.

I arrive at Silver Belles and am greeted by several patients rolling their wheelchairs through the halls. Some have gotten to know me, and I try to greet everyone I pass. One man always wears a Panama hat. Another man has attached a small American flag to his walker. It's been said many times, but nursing homes are some of the saddest places on earth.

As I walk to Gracie's room, I see where the staff has placed Halloween decorations throughout the building. There is an orange paper pumpkin with her name on her door. A black cat is pictured peeking from behind a gourd. I hope it is not a bad omen.

Gracie is waking up. She's groggy as she manages to greet me halfheartedly. "Is today Christmas?"

"No, Mom. It's almost Halloween. Max and Olivia are getting their costumes ready. They are all excited," I say, trying to bring some levity to her bad morning. "How are you feeling?"

"Did you bring me the money?"

"What money?"

"I won the lottery."

"No, you didn't. You don't have a ticket."

"Well then, did you bring the baubles?"

"No, Mom, I don't know about the baubles. What kind of baubles are they?"

"Garnets. And alabaster. Don't forget about the alabaster."

Gracie has now mentioned garnets. I found a man's garnet ring among her possessions, and the police found a bag of garnets, among other things, under the floor of my grandfather's cigar store. What more does she know? These dreams are real to her but disturbing to me. Many people with dementia think they have hidden wealth somewhere. Charisse told me her mother would hug her purse all day long during her last two years of life. But there may be some truth buried in there. She has now mentioned garnets. Why would she say that if she didn't have some past connection with them. I'm going to try to get her to give me more information.

"I'll look for the garnets," I say. "Where did you put them?"

"I can't remember."

"You just mentioned garnets. You must know something about them. Do you have some hidden away?"

"Papa has them. They are beautiful, but Mama doesn't like them."

"Did he put them in a safe? Are they in grandma's store?"

I look at Gracie and she has fallen back asleep. There's no need to try to talk to her. I'm going to leave.

Gracie has mentioned garnets so I know the gems are part of the mystery of Jefferson Bergstrom. I swing into the Steubenville Library and find Giana, the information associate. I tell her I'm looking for books on garnets. She checks the library's catalogue on her computer and directs me to several books on gems.

"These have to stay in reference so you can't take them home, but if there is anything else you need, just ask," Giana says.

"I'm doing some research on my family's genealogy," I say tentatively. "I'm kind of stumbling around with it."

"We have plenty of genealogy material available in our stacks and on our computers here in the library," she replies.

Giana turns to assist another patron, and I find a desk where I can search through two books on gems. I find that garnets are mined not just in New York but many states, including Pennsylvania, Vermont, and Idaho. In some cases, garnets are trapped in hard rock and found in open pits. Some are found in sedimentary sandstone. I already know from the Barton Mines that garnets are found along streams. I also know garnets are heavy and will sink to the bottom in water.

I learn that the name "garnet" comes from the Latin "granatum" meaning pomegranate. On my trip to Barton Mines I saw garnets that looked like clumps of pomegranate seeds molded together. Single garnets are transparent or translucent crystal. Most are red, but there are other colors too. The nicest garnets are selected to be made into jewelry. Once mined, they go to a lapidary (gem cutter) where they are sanded and polished. Egyptian pharaohs were sometimes buried with garnet necklaces to wear in the afterlife. Native Americans also used garnets in their ornaments. The gems are said to bring love and loyalty.

It can't be a coincidence that both of my grandfathers were involved with garnets. Jefferson Sr. was employed by a garnet mine, and Grandpa Gino had some in his possession through his "business"—probably nefariously. Could they have been used to pay off a bet? There must be a connection, and I'm going to find it.

I pack up my notebook and walk to the car. Before I can open the door I get a call from Bridgette. She sounds both perplexed and excited.

"I went to the doctor today and you'll never guess—I'm pregnant."

I'm glad I'm still standing and not driving—otherwise I might have wrecked my car. Bridgette is 40 years old. She had trouble getting pregnant and carrying the twins. I'm certain this was not planned.

"Well, this is a surprise. How is Joe taking the news?"

"He's thrilled, but we both know I must be careful. I'm going to cut back on some activities and get lots of rest."

"I'll help wherever I can. Just call me."

"But you are busy with Grandma Gracie."

"No problem. She's getting the best of care. You are my top priority now. Have you told the twins?"

"We're going to wait until after trick-or-treat night tomorrow. Do you want to come over? You can see the kids in their costumes."

"Better yet—I'll bring dinner," I reply. "You rest up. We'll talk tomorrow."

I hang up and wish for the thousandth time since his death that Anders were here. I now have a new set of worries. Bridgette won't be the first woman to get pregnant at age 40, and I know she has a good healthcare plan. She's physically in good shape. Still, I'll worry the whole way through this pregnancy.

I arrive home and for the first time since I was a teenager, I go to my jewelry box and find my rosary beads. There are some things in life you never forget. This is one of those. I light a candle and sit down. Silky comes and snuggles next to me. I take a deep breath and words tumble out. "Hail Mary…"

CHAPTER 14

I'm washing dishes after baking Halloween cupcakes for the twins and Gracie when my phone rings. I see that it is Kaylee Banks, the social worker at Silver Belles. She asks if I can stop in her office the next time I come by to double-check on a few things.

"I'm coming over to bring Gracie some cupcakes. I can be there in ten minutes," I say. She agrees, and I pack up the treats for the short trip.

Kaylee's office is decorated for Halloween with a picture on her door of a skeleton wearing a top hat. She greets me and we discuss Gracie's care plan. Kaylee suggests a few changes that my mother may like and a few I know she won't like. It is hard to get Gracie to attempt any activity because her cognitive abilities are so poor.

As I rise to leave, I spy a photo on Kaylee's desk of her at a Gore Mountain ski lodge that I recognize from my recent trip. I tell her that I have discovered my grandparents lived in North Creek and my father was born there.

"Really," she says, rather surprised. "There's great skiing around Gore Mountain. My sister lives in Glens Falls."

I sit back down and spend the next ten minutes going quickly through my mysterious family history and my desire to find a trace of why my grandfather moved there from Maine and whether Elin is still alive.

"My sister's best friend works at the *Chronicle*," Kaylee says. "I can ask if her friend can search through the paper's morgue for any info on your family. Tell me again the names you want researched."

I eagerly write down my grandparents' names, along with my father's and his sister Elin. I explain that I have no idea if she ever married. It may not be an easy search.

"I can't tell you how much this means to me," I say as I head to Gracie's room.

• • •

It's a crisp October evening for the pint-sized ghosts and goblins to be out prowling the neighborhood streets for candy. I arrive at Bridgette's house, and Max is dressed in a costume as Mario and Olivia as Princess Peach. I swear it is the cutest thing I've ever seen. Joe will be supervising their candy collections after they've eaten the dinner I've brought for them.

The kids are like two thoroughbreds pawing at the starting gate as the appointed time arrives for them to leave. Joe turns and smiles as he heads out, calling, "Wish me luck."

Bridgette and I post ourselves at her front door. In between our costumed porch visitors, I tell Bridgette the latest on my search for the Bergstroms.

"I also want to head back to Pittsburgh to do research on Native Americans in Pennsylvania and to search for Gracie's marriage certificate at the county courthouse. Want to go?"

Bridgette brightens at the suggestion. "Maybe I can take a personal day from school soon. I can use a break before I get too far along on this pregnancy. In a few months I may have to go on a medical leave of absence."

Bridgette says she will talk to her principal at school and call me tomorrow afternoon.

• • •

It's a sunny November day as Bridgette and I head to Pittsburgh. My car scatters dry leaves in a swirl as I go to pick up my daughter for our hour's drive to the Heinz History Center and to the Allegheny County Courthouse.

We decide to drive straight to Mt. Washington to view the historic bronze sculpture of George Washington and Guyasuta greeting each other at that spot over 250 years ago. We drive along Grandview Avenue before we cross the Ohio River. I motor down Grandview and find a side street to pull off and park. It's a short walk to the statue, but we find it is truly worthwhile. The sculpture, called Point of View, is amazing. From that high vantage point, you can see a sweeping view of downtown Pittsburgh. Its wide panorama reveals the point where east meets west. I can't help but think how important the forks of the Ohio are to American history. George Washington foresaw that his young nation's future would depend on land in the West, as he called the Ohio territory.

Guyasuta first became allied with Washington just before the start of the French and Indian War in 1754. The statue depicts them meeting in 1770 to examine land for future settlement along the Ohio River. The great clash of who was going to control the land was ready to begin.

Bridgette and I soak up the atmosphere for about fifteen minutes and head back to the car. "Let's go over to the Heinz Center now and see what we can find about our Seneca roots," I say, and Bridgette nods.

We pay our admission fee and head to the Detre Library & Archives inside the building. The library is a hands-on lab where students critically analyze material from their vast historical collection. The digitized archives are full of maps, manuscripts, and visual images. We both take notes on material pertaining to the Iroquois.

We next spend an hour going through an exhibit entitled "Clash of Empires: The British, French, & Indian War, 1754–1763" and are very impressed. I wish I had been able to take my history students here for a field trip, but it was too far to travel with them. Bridgette and I wrap up our time there by spending a half-hour on another exhibition on Lewis and Clark.

By now we both need a rest, so we go to the center's café for lunch. It feels good to get off our feet, and I check to make sure Bridgette isn't too tired. I know her different moods very well, and she seems fine, so I ask if she wants to head to the county courthouse or go home.

"Oh, let's go to the courthouse," she says. "I'm very curious to see what we can find on the marriage."

"Yes, and as Viviana used to say, *Mutto Bene.*"

We head inside the massive county courthouse to the marriage records office and hand over all the information we have on Gracie and Jefferson. Fifteen minutes later a clerk hands us a copy of a document dated June 6, 1959, confirming that my parents were married by a justice of the peace eight months before I was born. The witnesses are two people whose names I know very well, and I stare at the signatures with mounting anger—Carlton Bergstrom and Charisse Duhamel.

"Well, at least they got married and you were considered legitimate," Bridgette says, noting what an embarrassment that was for a woman in those days to be pregnant and unwed. "Still, I'll bet Great-Grandpa Gino and Great-Grandma Viviana were mad when they found out. No big Italian wedding for their daughter and no white wedding veil."

"No, only the shame of a pregnant offspring confessing her sins to her parents," I say. "That must have been a scene."

• • •

We are driving back to Steubenville, and I'm glad Bridgette is in the car with me so I can blow off steam. I'm having trouble coming to terms with the discovery that Charisse helped Gracie with her plan to elope back in 1959.

Damn, damn, damn. "I'm just crushed. I really am," I say in disgust. "This smells like the back end of a bean burrito. Charisse led me to believe she didn't know anything about Gracie's marriage plans. Her words to me were 'your mom and Jefferson left town together one weekend and came back married.' Why wouldn't she tell me the truth?"

"Mom, I think there's a simple explanation. Charisse is Gracie's best friend. Gracie probably begged her to plead ignorance on any mention of Jefferson or her brief marriage to him."

"I'd love to know what else she is hiding from me. What does she know about Jefferson's death? Had she been with him the night he died? Did Gracie talk to her as soon as she found out he was dead? Did the police interview Charisse about the homicide?"

"Mom, have you ever seen a copy of Jefferson's death certificate or the police report? I'm sure it is still in their cold case file."

"No, I've never seen it. Every time I go into the police station I get a case of hives."

"Didn't you tell me one of your former students is a Steubenville police officer?"

"Yes. Tim Konig."

"Contact him. Otherwise, you're going to drive yourself crazy."

"You're right. It doesn't hurt to ask. After this trip today, I'm determined to discover as much as I can. The case may not be solved, but it doesn't hurt to ask. I owe it to you and to myself to try my best."

"That's right, Mom. Gracie has kept too many secrets over the years. I've got two bright kids and a new little life coming along. No more secrets. We need to make things right."

CHAPTER 15

I'm groggy this morning as I stumble out to the kitchen with Silky on my heels. She doesn't spend too much time outside because it's cold. As I watch her skitter around the yard, I decide I'm going to confront Charisse about Gracie's wedding.

I pick up today's copy of the *Herald-Star* and wonder about the future of newspapers. The *Herald-Star* itself has quite a history behind it. In my position as a history teacher, I taught my students that one of the two founders of the paper in 1806 was John Miller. Six years after purchasing the paper, Miller was inspired to join the US Army to fight in the War of 1812. Four months later he was promoted to full colonel and took command of the Nineteenth Infantry. In this position, he fought in the Battle of Fort Meigs in northwest Ohio. He remained in the Army after the war and was assigned to Fort Bellefontaine in the Missouri Territory. By strange fate, he became the fourth governor of Missouri.

Meanwhile, James Wilson, grandfather of US President Woodrow Wilson, purchased the paper in 1815 and served for 23 years as proprietor and editor.

All kinds of information sources are now going to the internet, and print news is becoming extinct. What a change during my lifetime. American society has gone from print being the dominant news source in the country to it being a sad stepsister to reckless social media. A society that doesn't trust well-researched, legitimate news sources instead of raw opinions will be one in decline.

Grandpa Gino loved newspapers. Steubenville had a couple local reporters during the 1930s–1950s who poked their noses into Big G's Cigars on a regular basis. The word I heard from Gracie was he treated them like kings. He'd take them to the Naples Spaghetti House and feed them dinner and drinks. He also gave them tips on certain horses running at Wheeling Downs and other tracks. As a result, those reporters didn't dig too deeply into Big G's business. There were plenty of other crimes going on for them to fill their newsprint. The Jefferson County Courthouse was a very busy place.

I remember as a teenager reading about the time the KKK chapter from Wellsburg, West Virginia, appeared in the city. It alarmed everyone in town. Steubenville is also located close to other larger cities, and I-70 makes it an easy route for drug runners and human traffickers.

In the 1990s, the Steubenville police had a civil rights lawsuit filed against them, and the federal government came to investigate. Sometimes I feel like we are still paying for our past sins here. There was a time when there was a "numbers joint" in every neighborhood. Everyone gambled. You could walk in and bet a $5 baseball parlay as easily as you could buy a pack of gum. If things got "hot," you could always flee over the Market Street Bridge to West Virginia.

On the other hand, the city has some more heavenly aspects to it. There is a Fransiscan university here. It's also been known in the past as a city of churches. In addition, Steubenville is known for its murals. There are at least 25 of them in the downtown area. I like to think of all this as goodness amongst evil. The roses among the thorns, so to speak. It is my hometown. I've spent my career here as a wife, mother, grandmother, and teacher. Now I feel it's my duty to finish my work as a detective.

I snap out of my musings by the sound of my iPhone. I see I have an unknown caller from the Glens Falls area code.

"Hello, Mrs. Albrecht. I'm the sister of Kaylee Banks, who is the social worker at your mother's nursing home. I know you are trying to locate a relative. My friend who works at the *Chronicle* has tracked down a woman who might be a relative of yours living here in upstate New York."

"You don't know how much this means to me," I say.

"Let me add that the friend who got that phone number for you is well-connected here in town."

I'm stunned but thrilled by this conversation. I'm given the name, address, and phone number of Astrid Bergstrom's daughter Maja Lunden. The caller tells me that Maja is about 80 years old and lives in her own home.

My detective work is starting to click. Maja's mother would be my grandfather's sister. That makes Maja my great-aunt—an actual Bergstrom blood relative! I will attempt to call her later today. First, I must take care of business with Charisse.

• • •

Charisse is eating a bowl of Raisin Bran and watching *Judge Judy* on TV when I arrive. I called her on the way to her house with the premise of chatting about the Heinz History Center trip.

"Sit down, honey, and tell me all about it," she says. "Want some coffee before you start?"

I pass on the coffee and give her a description of the Point of View statue with George Washington and Guyusuta. I then segue into some of the info Bridgette and I learned about the Iroquois. Finally, I get to the real reason for the visit.

"Before going home, we went to the Allegheny County Courthouse."

"Oh."

"We were able to get a copy of Gracie's marriage certificate. You haven't told me the whole truth. Give it to me straight—no chaser."

Charisse slowly puts down her bowl of cereal and I see a tear start to well up in one eye.

"So, you know I was there," she confesses. "I'm so sorry I never told you, but it wasn't mine to tell."

"Do you realize how long I've searched for more info about my parents?" I ask, anger rising. "I've even asked you point blank, and you lied to me about where they were married. Why didn't you tell me?"

"Gracie made me swear that I'd never tell you."

"For God's sake, Charisse, can you imagine what it felt like for me to see Carlton's signature as a witness!"

I get up and pace around the living room squeezing my hands together and biting my lower lip.

"Mo, your mother made me swear. She is my lifelong best friend, and she is still alive. I planned to tell you once she is dead."

"What else can you tell me? Why did you go with Carlton to Pittsburgh?"

"We were dating at the time."

Again, I'm stunned. My brain feels numb. "And what else happened that weekend?"

"We drove to Monroeville east of Pittsburgh to a supper club called the Holiday House to celebrate the wedding. It was owned by friends of Sinatra's. Big singers like Tony Bennett, Al Martino, Mel Torme, Frankie Avalon, the Four Seasons, and Steubenville's own Dean Martin performed there. Even Connie Francis—she is one of my favorites. It was THE place to go for entertainment in these parts."

The book of matches that I found in Gracie's box. It was from there.

"We stayed all night and came home the next day. All four of us were so happy. That came to a screeching halt once we got back to Steubenville. Gracie had to face Big G and Viviana, and *la merda* hit the fan. Your grandmother dumped a warm plate of spaghetti down your father's *il cazzo*."

The spectacle of my angry grandmother flinging a pile of pasta on Jefferson's private parts makes me woozy.

"I'm going to process what you've told me. I may even go to church and light a candle. I'll call you later."

• • •

Whenever I am particularly tense, I turn to Johann Sebastian Bach. I like to think of him as my go-to composer to help ease my anxieties. He creates supernatural magic. I listen to his *Brandenburg*

Concerto No. 3 in G major and feel ready for the next big move in my life. I dial the phone number for Maja Lunden.

"Hello," a sweet elderly voice says into the phone.

"Is this Maja?" I say while tapping my foot nervously on the floor.

"Yes."

"I'm the daughter of Jefferson Bergstrom Jr. My grandfather was Jefferson Sr., son of Nils and Annika Bergstrom. Are you Astrid's daughter?"

"Yes!"

"My name is Maureen Albrecht, and you are my great-aunt."

"Oh, my Lord. Where are you?"

I tell Maja that I live an hour west of Pittsburgh along the Ohio River in a small town called Steubenville. I explain some of the background on my parents and that Jefferson died before I was born. I specifically don't mention the suspected poisoning and that Carlton is the alleged perpetrator. I simply want to break through the initial contact with my newly found Bergstrom relative.

"I tell you what, Maureen," Maja says. "I have a niece who lives in Greensburg, Pennsylvania, east of Pittsburgh. Her name is Sonja Lunden. Let me give her a call and I'll ring you back."

"Promise?"

"Sure thing. You are a Bergstrom. I've always wondered what happened to you after your father died."

Her words are music to my ears. I take a deep breath. Will she call me back or is she just trying to get me off the phone? I return to Bach and listen to "St. Matthew Passion."

Silky is jumping around, demanding a walk. I check the outdoor temperature on my iPhone, and it is not too bad for mid-November. I zip up my coat, put on a wool hat, and head down the street with Silky on a leash. My neighbors honk and wave, and Silky wags her tail. We spot a squirrel, and of course, Silky wants to chase it. Just as she pulls as hard as she can against the leash, my phone rings. It looks like the Pittsburgh area code. Excitement wells as I anticipate another big moment in my life.

Before I can answer the call, Silky pulls away from the leash and sends my phone flying. It lands in the street five feet from the curb. I'm instantly torn between retrieving the phone or trying to catch Silky. Just then a cement truck tools along the street and rolls over my phone. My heart sinks as I hear a sickening sound of one of technology's greatest inventions being crushed under truck tires. I run after Silky, grab her by the collar, and scoot her back toward my phone. The front of my iPhone is cracked beyond recognition. All I want to do is sit on the curb and cry out (as Grandma Viviana would do), *Maledizioni* (curses).

CHAPTER 16

Sometimes I feel like I'm a character in Kenneth Grahame's children's book *The Wind in the Willows*. I picture myself as Mr. Toad in his motor car during one of Toad's wild rides. I'm driving past Pittsburgh on my way to a small town in western Pennsylvania called Greensburg. Right now, I'm passing close to Monroeville—the site of Holiday House where my parents spent their honeymoon night. But my real destination is the Laurel Highlands where about 20 of my Bergstrom relatives have invited me to Thanksgiving dinner.

How did I get this lucky? After the cement truck wrecked my cell phone, I took it to the store where I had purchased it. A tech savvy salesman was able to transfer my contact list onto another iPhone. Less than 24 hours after its demise, I was using a replacement phone to call Sonja Lunden, a Bergstrom cousin. She seemed intrigued with my story and invited me to join some long-lost relatives for the big feast.

The Laurel Highlands have the highest mountains in Pennsylvania. Greensburg is 55 miles southeast of Pittsburgh and is home to Seton Hill University and the Westmoreland Museum of Art. I was told by Sonja that her husband is a professor at the university and she works at the museum.

My route has taken me along I-376 past the Monroeville area to I-76 south and Route 30 east to Greensburg. I make note that there's a casino in the area in case I need to have Charisse accompany me someday. My plan is to stay overnight in a local hotel and return to Steubenville tomorrow.

I'm approaching Greensburg (pop. 14,976) and am enjoying the beauty of the landscape. In certain ways it reminds me of Gore Mountain in that there is plenty of hiking and camping. Even more pertinent is the fact the trout fishing here is supposed to be terrific. As was the case in September, I suddenly feel the weight of losing both Toby and Anders. I will certainly tell Joe about this place in case he ever wants to bring the kids here.

The closer I get to the house, the more nervous I become. I need to pee, so I pull into a fast-food restaurant and use their facilities. Thanks to my car's GPS system, I approach my destination and find the home of my Thanksgiving host Sonja Lunden. I see a beautiful 2-story stone house before me. The lawn is immaculate, with a stone walkway complete with runway lights. Several small children are zooming around the yard, kicking a soccer ball and wearing shorts and jackets. Am I really within 25 feet of a house full of Bergstroms? Is this real or am I in Oz?

I ring the doorbell and am swept into an exhilarating maelstrom of Nordic hospitality. There are three generations of Bergstrom descendants present. Sonja ushers me around to meet her husband, two sons, and their wives. Assorted children scurry by as Sonja takes me into a back room overlooking a large patio with an outdoor kitchen brushing up against a wooded lot. Bird feeders dot the backyard. Everything appears tranquil. There I meet another Bergstrom relative—a man named Fredrik Lunden. He introduces himself as Maja's son and Sonja's brother.

"My dear sister goes by her maiden name," he says, grinning. "Otherwise, she'd have to use her husband's German surname Huhnerbein. It translates to 'chicken leg.'"

Sonja jabs him playfully in the side and asks him to pour me a drink. "Please treat your newfound cousin with Swedish hospitality while I check on the meal," Sonja says to him, then turns to me. "My brother is the official family historian. He loves to talk about the Bergstroms. So happy you are here, Maureen."

Fredrik pours me a glass of Riesling and tells me to call him Fred. I look around the room and see a framed Swedish flag over a fireplace with a banner saying *Valkommen*. Fred tells me everything he knows about our great-grandparents Nils and Annika Bergstrom.

"Let's start at the beginning. They both had connections to Vasterbottens County in northern Sweden," he begins. "It borders the Norwegian county of Nordland on the west and the Gulf of Bothnia on the east. Annika was born in Robertsfor in Vasterbottens County. We think Annika's father worked in an iron factory. That area has lots of iron mines. Nils's father was born in Vindeln in Vasterbottens County."

Fred tells me that both Nils's parents and Annika's parents wanted to make a new life in the US. They all came through Ellis Island and immediately headed to Maine, a state that had recruited Swedes since 1870 to live in a colony called New Sweden. Nils and Annika were part of the second generation of immigrants to live there. By then Maine's sister villages of Westmanland and Stockholm were beginning to grow. I've been up there for their Midsommar celebration and it's a real treat. You should go."

Fred asks me about my background, and I explain that I'm a retired history teacher. He seems delighted with this news. As much as I long to hear more about the Bergstrom family, he wants to ask me about Ohio history and its role in the Civil War. Just as I start to explain about Abe Lincoln and Salmon P. Chase, an Ohio governor who served as his secretary of the treasury, we are called to dinner.

"I want to talk about General William Tecumseh Sherman after dinner," he says with a wink. I promise that I will.

The dinner starts off with a toast and a hearty "Skol!" I look around at my fair-haired cousins and can almost picture them in Viking ships sailing off on grand adventures. The children get bored after dessert and run back outside to play before the sun sets. I notice that one of the boys has a plastic Viking hat on as he runs past the window.

I explain that I am staying at the local Holiday Inn Express and will leave tomorrow morning after a strong cup of coffee.

"No, please come back in the morning and we'll talk more. It's less than two hours back to Steubenville from here. Maybe we can squeeze in a trip to Historic Hanna's Town. It dates from 1773 and was the first seat of government for Westmoreland County. It also had the first English courts west of the Allegheny Mountains. It's right down your alley. You'll love it."

• • •

I've had a good night's sleep at the hotel and am looking forward to spending this morning with my Bergstrom cousins without the confusion of the children. Sonja's brother Fred is staying with her until Saturday and driving back to Glens Falls. He invites me to come to upstate New York and meet his mother next summer and bring my family.

"I would love to do that," I say. "I fell in love with Gore Mountain when I visited in September. My daughter and her husband have an RV, and I'll ask if they would like to go camping. I would also love to meet your mother."

"She's 80 now and not quite as sharp as she once was," Fred says, "but you'd like her."

Sonja insists we three get in her car and go to the historic village which took up arms against Great Britain and supported Boston. We explore the reconstructed Hanna Tavern, fort, and "gaol" (jail). By the time we finish our tour, it is noon.

"It has been great to be here," I say, "but I really need to get back home. As you know, the weather in November can get tricky, and it will be dark by 5 o'clock."

Sonja drives me back to get my car and I ask how Maja is doing health-wise. I then work up enough courage to ask my cousins the question that's been foremost on my mind. "Has your mother ever mentioned if she knows what happened to my father after he left Glens Falls and went into the army?"

"I did call her last night to report on our reunion," Sonja says. "She can remember seeing Jefferson Jr. once in Glens Falls while he was home on leave visiting his parents. She said after the army your father went to Harrisburg, Pennsylvania, and worked in a nightclub. Eventually word trickled back that he died in

Steubenville in 1960. So sad about your father. I'm glad we are now connected."

"Me too," I say. "Please stay in touch."

• • •

I pull my car into a parking space at Silver Belles and head inside. The staff is beginning to put up Christmas decorations. I get to Gracie's doorway and I see Charisse sitting in a chair next to my mother's bed. It's obvious Charisse brought her lunch.

"Hello ladies," I say cheerfully.

"Hi Mo," Charisse replies. "I thought your mom could use some company today. We've been talking."

"Did you two talk about going to the Gold Mine?" I ask.

"Yes," Gracie says brightly. "Char and I are going tomorrow. We are going to dance all night."

I stare at Charisse in disbelief. They must have been reminiscing about their teenage years.

"We had some good times, didn't we Gracie," Charisse says.

"Dad doesn't know we go there," Gracie says, still thinking she is living in 1958. "I'm hoping Jefferson and Carlton will be there."

I'm shocked. My mother has never spoken either of their names, let alone both together. Her mind is getting worse or she wouldn't have done it. Charisse gets up to leave, and I ask if she could talk to me in the hall for a moment. She nods, and I tell Gracie I'll be right back.

"How did you know about the Gold Mine?" Charisse asks me when Gracie can't hear us.

"I found some stuff in Gracie's belongings, and I did some research," I reply. "Did both my father and Carlton live in Beaver Falls?"

"Jefferson worked there. Carlton came to visit him right before the Christmas of 1958," Charisse explains. "They both showed up here in Steubenville one day and told us to come up to the Gold Mine. Gracie and I went the next weekend, and the two couples got along great. I started dating Carlton, and your mom started dating Jefferson. Each Friday the boys would come to Steubenville, then head home to Beaver Falls on Sunday nights. We had only been dating for six months when Jefferson and Gracie got married. Your grandparents were furious. Jefferson and Gracie got an apartment, and Carlton took over Jefferson's job. Jeff went to work for Big G."

I start to ask another question when I hear a yowl coming from Gracie's room. We run in and see that Gracie has fallen out of bed. A small pool of blood puddles near her head. She starts to moan.

Nursing personnel descend on the room, and Charisse and I step outside so they can attend to Gracie. "I've been expecting this to happen," I say.

"She was probably trying to follow us when we left the room," Charisse says. "She doesn't realize anymore that she can't walk."

"God only knows where this will lead."

CHAPTER 17

Gracie is drifting in and out of consciousness, and there is not anything I can do. I sit at her bedside for several hours but feel growing anxiety at my inability to help. I decide to do something to pass the time—I head over to the Steubenville library.

Maja Lunden had informed me that my father had once lived in Harrisburg and worked at a nightclub. I'm going to spend some time learning more about life in Pennsylvania's capital city.

I go to my favorite information associate, Giana, and ask her about Harrisburg, Pennsylvania. She grins at me and says, "Are you writing a travelogue?"

"No, just doing some family research," I reply.

"You must have an interesting family."

Giana guides me to a section of the library where I can dig into a few books. "If you need to look things up on our computers, let me know," she says and heads off to assist another patron.

The first thing that catches my eye is the fact there is gold mining in Lebanon, York, and Lancaster Counties to the south and east of Harrisburg, especially in the small towns of Dillsberg, Grantham, and Wellsville. The Susquehanna River runs through Harrisburg, and from what I can tell, gold flakes and nuggets have been found in many places along the riverbeds. It seems that ice age glacial drifts deposited placer gold along these areas thousands of years ago.

York County, for one, is a good place for a beginner bitten by the gold bug. From what I can read, Lancaster County near the towns of Quarryville and Peter's Creek is another good location. Of particular interest is the Cornwall Iron Mine in Cornwall, where thousands of ounces of gold are collected as a byproduct of iron mining.

I stop and ponder this for a minute. Do you suppose my father took his knowledge of mining from the Barton Mines in North River and applied it to a search for gold in southeastern Pennsylvania? Could this possibly be true? It is as good of a theory as anything I have right now, so I turn back to my research on his possible employment at a Harrisburg jazz club.

I find that jazz in Harrisburg was very popular in the 1950s and on across the 1960s. Unknown to me, both Pittsburgh and Philadelphia made contributions to the evolution of jazz, with Harrisburg geographically sandwiched in between. Even the most casual fan of jazz, like me, knows that Creole, ragtime, and blues had an influence on it.

Both my Grandmother Viviana and Gracie liked jazz. Viviana was delighted to watch Louis Armstrong on TV, and Gracie would often sing or hum Paul Desmond's *Take Five*, which some call the greatest single record in jazz history.

Could it be that I got my interest in music from my father? Why would he work in a jazz club if he didn't like music?

I find Giana and ask for the password to use one of the library's computers. I look up Harrisburg's newspaper—*The Patriot-News*. I see that it started in 1820. The area where Harrisburg sits was once inhabited by Native Americans, who found it a natural crossroad to trails that led to both the Ohio River and the Delaware River.

Harrisburg was originally known as Harris' Ferry in 1785, named after English trader John Harris Sr. It reached its peak in population (almost 90,000) in the 1950s—the same time my father moved there. I can see photos on the newspaper's website of the town in its heyday. It seems the place was quite lively—a good place for a young man fresh from the military to get a job in the entertainment industry. No doubt Pennsylvania politicians working in their capital city could enjoy the nightlife without traveling 100 miles to its big brother Philadelphia.

I scour the *Patriot-News* for nightclubs. I see that currently there are 30 of them in town. It's not Las Vegas but not bad for eastern Pennsylvania. But I want to search for those nightclubs from the 1950s. I start to dig in when my phone rings. It's Gracie's nurse at Silver Belles, and she needs me to stop by. I better leave.

• • •

I walk into Gracie's room and see that she is somewhat alert. Part of her head is bandaged, and she is sitting up and trying to communicate.

"Please stay," Gracie mumbles as I pull up a chair next to her bed.

"I'll eat supper with you and we'll watch TV together. *The People's Court* is on soon."

She attempts a slight smile and dozes off again. I ask the staff to bring an extra tray for me to eat at dinner. To kill time, I call Bridgette and give her a report.

"Gracie wants me to stay for a while. I'll wait until about 8:00 p.m. and then I'll go home," I say.

"Do you need for me or Joe to go feed Silky and let her go out in the backyard?"

"No, she should be okay," I say.

"Come on, Mom. She can't last that long. I'm sending Joe anyway. Tell Grandma Gracie that we love her."

I sink back into the chair and prepare myself to sit through another three hours of what I call "nursing home blues." The constant din of nursing carts, wheelchairs, food trolley, wandering visitors, noisy children, maintenance personnel, delivery men, and confused patients looking for their rooms is anything but restful. I flip on Gracie's TV and hear Christmas jingles in commercial after commercial.

I think about my interrupted research into Harrisburg's nightclubs. I pick up my iPhone and go to an online shopping store where I have an account. Within seconds I order a book called *The History of Harrisburg Nightlife*. It should arrive in a week.

Gracie starts to stir. I remind her I am still here. At first she thinks she is in her home in Mingo Junction, then realizes she is still at Silver Belles. She frowns.

"They put you in here and then you go crazy because you can't get out. Then you're so crazy there is no chance you can get out," she sighs. "There's nothing else to do but die."

I get up at 7:30 a.m. and look out my bedroom window. It's snowing. I take my time eating breakfast and reading the *Herald-Star*. I'm in no hurry to visit Gracie. At 9:00 a.m. I receive a call from Charisse. It's early for her to be up, so I hope she does not have an emergency.

"Mo, how's your mom?" she asks anxiously. "I've hardly slept thinking about her."

"I was with her until 8:00 p.m. I'm not going to lie—she's depressed."

"I don't want to drive my car today, but if you're going to go see her, will you pick me up?"

"Sure. We'll get her a milkshake and eat lunch with her."

Charisse seems relieved, and we hang up. I grab Gracie's copy of the book *A Coney Island of the Mind* and put it in my purse. I'm going to ask Charisse about the poem.

• • •

I roll my car up to Charisse's condo and she wades slowly through four inches of snow to my car. I greet her warmly. "Did you have any problems walking in the snow?"

"Have you ever seen a duck walk in stilettos?" she laughs.

I pull out *Coney Island*, chapter 8. "I found this book recently in Gracie's desk," I say. "A few months ago, I discovered someone had copied this same poem and given it to her. The note is handwritten and signed with only an initial 'C.' Can you recall if you ever wrote that down when the two of you were reading beat literature in the 1950s?"

Charisse thinks for a second. I know she won't lie about this one. "No, Maureen. I honestly can tell you I never copied it. We each dabbled in writing some poor imitations of beat poets, but I never copied the works of famous writers like Ferlinghetti. You must remember, we were just dumb kids when we did that, and in hindsight, we never should have gone to the Gold Mine."

"I believe you, Charisse. Don't feel bad. If you two had not gone there and Mom had not met Jefferson, I wouldn't be here. Did Gracie ever date someone who had a first name that started with 'C'?"

"The only one I can think of is Chip Hanover, whose son Mike works on your car at Hanover Auto Repairs. Gracie and Chip dated several times and went to the senior dance together. He left to go into the navy as soon as we graduated. I don't think they ever wrote to each other, but as you know, we all have stayed friends all these years."

"Next time I need work on my car I'll take the original note with me," I say. "I'll ask Mike."

• • •

I'm driving my old Dodge Caravan in the slush of snow that mucks up the streets in downtown Steubenville this time of year. It's messy during the day when the temperature rises enough to melt the snow into dirty slush but later freezes into a slippery obstacle course when the sun goes down. That's the part of winter in Ohio I dislike.

But the worst thing about driving in the cold is the potholes. The freezing and thawing of Ohio's winters causes the blacktop to break down, and the city's pothole patrol must fill them temporarily with patching material until new asphalt can be made in May. It's even worse when a pothole fills with snow and you don't know it's there.

Sure enough, while heading to the mall to do some Christmas shopping, I hit the Grand Canyon of potholes. My Caravan jerks and groans and immediately I feel a wobble like I've never felt while driving. I'm hoping I haven't broken an axle.

I'm not far from Hanover's Auto Repair, and I cross my fingers that I can get there. Luckily Mike is on duty and gives my car an inspection.

"You're going to have to leave it overnight," he says. "The axle is not broken, but your rim is bent badly. I'll replace it. Call Joe and have him pick you up."

Mike tells me to come and sit in his office. This will give me an opportunity to ask my questions. I rummage through my purse and pull out the note with the *Coney Island* poem written on it.

"Charisse Duhamel told me your father dated Gracie a couple times during high school. This is a copied poem someone, probably a boyfriend, wrote to her. By any chance, does this look like your dad's handwriting?"

Mike looks at it and laughs. "Well, first—Dad is not a sentimental man. Two—he hates poetry. Three—he never uses cursive. He always prints his words."

"I see," I say. "It was a long shot. I'm just trying to solve the mystery of my father's brief life in Steubenville. Gracie won't talk about it, and now she could be dying."

"Sorry to hear that," Mike says. "I'll tell my dad. He mentions Gracie often. She and Charisse are the only two women from their class who still live here. He always felt Gracie got a bum rap with her husband being killed."

I wait for Joe, who soon arrives and immediately inspects my damaged tire. I get in Joe's car, and Mike motions for me to roll down the passenger window.

"If you'd like to visit with Dad, I'll give him a call. I don't know if you ever went out there like Anders and I did when we were younger, but Dad lives south of Mingo on Route 151. It's the area where that mysterious fire burned down a church about 20 years ago. There's not much out there, but they still call the area by its old nickname—Brimstone."

CHAPTER 18

It's cold outside, but the sun is bright and the sky is blue—unusual for eastern Ohio in the first week of December. Everything is nearly ready for Christmas on my part, including presents for Gracie, so I take advantage of the weather and call Chip Hanover and ask if I can pay him a visit. He is thrilled that I am coming to see him.

Marvin 'Chip' Hanover had been kind enough to come to the funeral home right before Anders's memorial service. Chip had dressed up in a suit and tie, which was certainly far from his normal attire. He told me he enjoyed the times Anders and Mike spent at his house flying radio-controlled airplanes or going hunting for deer in the fall during their youth.

I have never been to the Hanover farm, but I certainly know my way around Mingo Junction and to the spot where Route 151 dovetails into the southern edge of town. I head west and follow Mike Hanover's instructions. I look for a bare blacktop parking lot where the county sometimes stores large equipment when working on the roads. Until 20 years ago a white framed church stood on the grounds. It proudly welcomed parishioners for five decades until a mysterious fire burned it to the ground. No one was ever charged, but the nickname Brimstone stuck.

I soon pass a low brick apartment building with three front doors—a triplex. It's unusual to see that kind of building out here in the countryside, but there it sits. Mike had instructed me to look for his dad's driveway just beyond a sign that says *Apartment for Rent* with a phone number.

I pull into a long ribbon of a driveway with a slight incline. I see a well-kept farmhouse with a veranda across the front. As I drive closer I see two rocking chairs near the front door—true Americana. I grab my gifts of a tin of homemade Christmas cookies, a fruit basket, and a 12-pack of Little Kings Cream Ale. Chip Hanover sees me through his front window and comes outside.

"Good to see you again," I say as he meets me near the porch steps.

"Welcome to Brimstone!" Chip replies.

"Your son says you are a Little Kings connoisseur."

"Some beer drinkers say it has a skunky flavor," he laughs, "but I love it. They stopped brewin' it for a while but it's back. They can't keep a good beer down."

We go inside and Chip tells me he has made coffee. "I know ladies like tea, but I don't drink it—I think it tastes like piss, pardon my French. Do you take cream or sugar?"

"No, just black and bitter," I say. "You didn't have to make coffee for me, but I'll certainly take a cup. It's chilly outside."

We talk about Mike and his son Ralphie and how well the business is doing. Then we reminisce about Anders, and I tell him my grandson Max reminds me of my husband.

"Max likes radio-controlled airplanes just like Anders. It's too bad Anders became ill before Max was old enough for the two of them to fly planes together. But Joe loves them too, so the tradition goes on."

Eventually our conversation turns to Gracie.

"Charisse told me that you took Gracie to your senior dance back in the day. Is that right?"

"Yep. We went out a few times—nothing serious. Boy oh boy, Gracie and Charisse—them two gals were always jokin' and laughin'. We were buddies. I knew I wanted to go into the navy as soon as I got out of high school, so I signed with a recruiter in February and shipped out right after graduation. My folks didn't get along very well, and I was tired of hearin' them fight."

"Did you come back to the farm when you left the navy?"

"Yep. My pappy had a heart attack so the navy gave me an early out. I took care of our beef cattle and worked as a mechanic in town to support my folks. As soon as Pap died in 1961, my mama scooted out of town to go live with her sister in Chillicothe. She hated farm life."

"How did you meet your wife?"

"She's from Weirton but came to Steubenville to work at the Jefferson County Courthouse. She brought her car to the shop one day, and I asked her for a date. You probably know she died of cancer around the same time as Anders. Damn cancer," he hisses.

I tell Chip that his home is lovely, and he asks if I would like a tour.

"Sure, but one quick question," I say. "You may remember that Gracie and Charisse were really enthralled by jazz and the beat poets of the 1950s during high school. Did you, perchance, ever copy down a poem from the book *A Coney Island of the Mind* and give it to Gracie as a gift?"

Chips lets out a belly laugh and shakes his head. "Nope, the only coney I know is the one with sauce and onions you eat at the fair. I don't think I've ever even read a poem."

"I just had to ask. I'm trying to put pieces of Gracie's past together before she dies."

"She's a good soul," he says. "Let me show you around."

Chip tells me his fireplace is made from stones found on the property. The kitchen is large, with lots of cabinets. Surprisingly, there is a modern stove and beautiful kitchen curtains. A shelf with fine china cups and saucers sits to the right of the large farm sink.

"My wife liked to cook and sew," Chip says proudly. Then he asks if I would like to see the upstairs. "Your father and grandpap have a slight connection to this place. I can show you if you like."

My curiosity is off the charts as we climb up the carpeted stairs to the upper floor. I can see three rooms with beds covered in lovely quilts. "My wife made them things," he says. "Occasionally I have a boarder who uses one of the rooms up here. I also own that triplex at the end of the lane. Profits from them apartments help keep the farm runnin'."

He takes me to the doorway of one room and points. "See that dressin' table with the big round mirror? There's a door behind it. My pap used to hide moonshine there for friends. He would meet his customers in the church parkin' lot to make the exchange. He hid plenty of 'shine for your grandpap over the years."

"Oh, wow," I stammer. "I'm not surprised."

"Then in late '58 and most of '59 your father would stop out here and rent space for some of his valuables."

I gulp. "I imagine that could have been most anything."

"He had another storage space in the barn if you want to see it."

We grab our coats and head across the gravel lot to the large barn. I see Chip's herd of cattle roaming around a muddy field, enjoying a rare moment of December sunshine. Chip points up to the top of the barn and says he bales and stores his own hay in the hayloft with the help of his son and grandson. He slides open a big barn door wide enough for the two of us to pass inside and shows me around. I see several stalls, and he tells me his dad once had two draft horses. He also says that Mike once had a barrel horse and used to ride it in competitions.

"Do you still board horses?"

"Not anymore," he laughs. "I just board people, either in the house or in the triplex."

"I see one of the stalls is a tack room."

"Yep. To earn some extra income years ago, my pap dug a big hole under these floorboards and rented out storage space for selected customers," he said with a wink. "Jefferson Bergstrom was one of Pap's last customers before his heart attack. Once pap died, I discontinued this part of the enterprise and concentrated on the cattle, the triplex, and my auto repair business."

"Could I see the storage space?" I ask bravely.

"'Suppose so. It will be dusty, so beware."

Chip pulls back a worn rug, which reveals a hidden hinged door with a brass pull-tab ring. He lifts the door and grabs a flashlight. "It should be empty, but let's see."

Chip points his light down into the hole, and I'm surprised to see it is quite large. A man could stand up to his waist in it. "I can't tell you what all was hidden in here—that was Pap's business."

Luckily I see no rodents and smell no obnoxious odors. I spot an old grain sack hidden in a corner. It's partially covered with dirt. "What's that?" I point.

"Who knows? Too small for a dead body," he laughs. "Let me yank it out."

Chip hops in the hole and, with one swing, grabs the sack and throws it onto the hard floor. It lands with a thump. He pulls out a pocketknife and cuts a rope that ties the sack together. Out tumbles a smaller cloth bag and a gun.

"Well," Chips says. "What have we here?" He picks up the gun and checks the chamber to see if it is loaded. "Nope, it's empty."

The gun looks all too familiar. "May I see it for a second?" I ask. I bravely turn it over and back. "Big G had one just like it."

"Could be his," Chip says. "I know he was a customer, although he usually had a runner bring things out here. Let's see what's in this bag."

Chip opens the cloth bag and out pours a big pile of garnets. I suck in my breath.

"That's pretty unusual for out here in Brimstone," he says.

"If we can go back in the house," I stammer. "I have a story for you."

. . .

I feel exhaustion hovering over me as I go back inside Chip's house. I tell him the Steubenville police have given me Gino's other Glock and that they are holding another bag of garnets.

"I suspect they have more items," I say. "The police told me they consider my father's death a cold case never solved. I know they have more they're not telling me. It doesn't help that Jefferson's death was 62 years ago. I'm trying my hardest to do some detective work, but I'm such an amateur."

"Mo, just keep diggin'," Chip says in a fatherly way. "I try to keep my nose out of other people's business. But with Gracie in such bad shape, your best bet is to keep after Charisse. She's very loyal to your mama, but she probably knows more than she's tellin' you. It was a terrible thing that happened to your father—you never got to know him. Poor Gracie. She plum didn't deserve that."

I get back in my car and head down the lane and out to Route 151. I pass the triplex and realize the old rental sign has Chip's phone number on it. I wonder how long the triplex has been there?

I come to Mingo Junction and remember I need to go to Gracie's house and check on a few things. I'm mentally spent right now, so I'm going to go home. Gracie's house is becoming a burden and I need to sell it. Why haven't I done so?

The winter sun is slowly easing its way into the horizon as I pull into my driveway. Silky is very happy to see me, but first she wants to run in the backyard. While she bounces around in an old snow drift I go to my mailbox. I retrieve what looks like two Christmas cards and the book I ordered on Harrisburg nightlife.

I feed Silky and finally plop into my comfy chair. I open the package, and sure enough it is the Harrisburg book. I leaf through the pages and promise myself I will read it tomorrow. I start to put it down, but I turn one more page. Sure enough, an image catches my eye. Page 25—a black-and-white photo shows a fair-haired man with a catchy smile next to another man holding a saxophone. The caption reads, *Jefferson Bergstrom, stage manager for the Bogalusa Club, is seen with musician "Suggs" Slidell before a show. Both men served in the same US Army unit while stationed at Fort Stewart in Georgia.*

CHAPTER 19

Christmas with Bridgette and her family is lovely. After dinner I take a plate of food to Gracie at Silver Belles. She picks at it but is disinterested. Instead, she asks me again if she could have rye toast with cheese on it. I try to get her to open her presents, but she just stares at them.

"What are these?" she asks me. When I tell her Santa brought them, she sets the gifts aside and promptly falls asleep.

• • •

Today is New Year's Eve. I've been stewing all week about what to do with the second Glock in my possession. I know it is unloaded, and of course, I own no bullets so it can't hurt anyone. For now, it is hidden under my kitchen sink.

I decide to give Maja Lunden a call and wish her Happy New Year. Her daughter, my newfound cousin Sonja Lunden, had told me she gave her mother a full report on our Thanksgiving weekend reunion. Sonja added that her mother would love to meet me if I come to Glens Falls. She rarely travels anymore due to problems with arthritis.

Maja answers on the second ring. She is happy to hear from me. I jokingly ask her if she is going to party at Poopies Diner in Glens Falls tonight, and she laughs. "They don't serve lutefisk," Maja replies, "and they're closed for dinner."

I tell her about my grandkids and that my daughter is pregnant again at age 40. I add that Bridgette must rest as much as possible and will probably have to go on a leave of absence from teaching. The baby is due in June.

"Oh, a new Bergstrom relative," Maja says. "How wonderful!"

We chat about several things, and then I zero in on my biggest question. "Can you tell me anything about my grandfather? I know he was sick when he arrived in Glens Falls."

"I was only about 10 years old when your grandparents and Elin moved here from North Creek," Maja says. "My mother had some nurse's training, so she helped with his care. He also got some treatments at a veteran's clinic because he was in the army reserves during World War II."

Maja proceeds to tell me my grandfather had some sort of autoimmune disease, which she describes as "something like Lupus." "His face would swell, and he would get red rashes on his body. He was in a wheelchair most of the time because his joints ached so."

I ask if my grandparents lived close to her house. Maja replies that they rented a tiny one-bedroom house about four blocks away.

"Elin slept on a Murphy bed, which as a kid, I thought was cool. She was four years older than I was, so we were not close. As soon as she graduated from high school, she moved away."

"Do you still have contact with her?" I ask.

"No, the last I knew she had gotten married and lives somewhere in eastern Pennsylvania. I think she has a daughter."

Pennsylvania. My DNA test showed another female relative from that state other than Sonja.

"Your grandfather died of kidney failure associated with Lupus," Maja said. "It was very sad."

"What about my grandmother?" I ask. "I know nothing about her."

"Oh, Eleanora was so sweet. She took good care of your grandfather and would spend time cooking things he might like. She even experimented with a few herbal cures."

"Was she able to work to help support them?"

"Eleanora was a wonderful seamstress. She made special dresses for many of the women in the area. I still have the prom dress she made me. But it doesn't fit anymore," she laughs.

We chat for a few more minutes and I decide not to push her for any other information.

"Happy New Year," I say. "I'm glad we could talk."

"Feel free to call again," Maja says. "I have nothing much else to do."

• • •

Bridgette has invited me over for New Year's Day dinner. It was a tradition in my Grandma Viviana's family that they always ate lasagna and garlic bread to start the new year right. Anders used to joke that garlic wards off evil spirits. Each January, when Gracie continued with this tradition, he would tease her about Italians and garlic.

As Bridgette works in the kitchen, it gives me an opportunity to tell her about my conversation with Maja. I tell her what she revealed about my grandfather's Lupus.

"I spent a couple hours last night looking up immune system illnesses. There are several autoimmune diseases—Raynaud's syndrome, Sjogren's syndrome, Hashimoto's disease, hypothyroidism, and others. I certainly hope Max doesn't develop any of these, but I think it's worth telling his doctors that there may be a genetic link."

"That's good to know, Mom," Bridgette says. "Max is doing pretty well right now, but it's something I worry about all the time."

"Let's all eat extra garlic tonight and hope for the best," I say.

"We're going to need it, Mom. I just found out yesterday I am carrying twins again."

• • •

Last night Bridgette gave me two pieces of lasagna and garlic bread to take home—one for Gracie and one for me. I decide to take them to Silver Belles today, where I can warm them up and have lunch with Gracie.

I step into the lobby and wish the receptionist a belated Happy New Year. I enter my mother's room and see she is dozing in a Broda chair in front of her TV. *The View* is blaring at full volume, with women yelling at each other. Gracie doesn't stir.

"Mom, I'm here," I say gently. No reaction.

I tap her on the shoulder. She opens one eye at half-mast. "Oh," she says. "It's you."

"Bridgette made Viviana's lasagna for you. Let's have lunch together."

"Who's Bridgette?"

I'm stunned. This has never happened before. I realize Gracie is getting worse. "Let's eat," I say.

"No. I need to find Carlton."

I feel like a grenade has exploded in the room. "Carlton?" I stammer.

"Yes, Mo. I'm dying. Find Carlton."

• • •

I'm chewing on my lips as hard as I can without drawing blood. What do I do? I try to summon Grandma Viviana from the past and wonder what she would do in this situation. Viviana was always very stoic in tense situations. Most likely she would say "the past is past—don't go back." Still, my mother wants to know what happened to Carlton. Why?

I get inside my Caravan and head down the street, creating a plan at each stop light. The office of the *Herald-Star* is only a few blocks away. I'm going to gamble at my own casino and hope for a big payoff.

I pull into the newspaper parking lot and find a receptionist inside the building. I muster as much charm as I can. "Do you have old editions on microfilm that I can access?"

The receptionist leads me to a side room, and I tell her I'm looking to search for papers from November and December 1959.

"Here you go," she says. "You can also access them online."

I thank her and dig in. I scroll through several rolls and, sure enough, I hit the jackpot.

> *Steubenville police report a man was found dead in the Rosewood apartment building on Dec. 1. The body of Jefferson Bergstrom Jr. was discovered after neighbors called police to report a disturbance in the early morning hours. Bergstrom was last seen at 2 a.m. at Post-Time Recreation in the company of his cousin Carlton Bergstrom. Witnesses stated both men engaged in an altercation with another patron. Police are investigating the murder. Jefferson Bergstrom was employed at Big G's Cigars. The business is owned by his father-in-law, Gino Rivers. He is survived by his pregnant wife, Gracie.*

I hand the microfilm back to the receptionist and head to the parking lot. I half walk, half trot to my car with my head throbbing and my stomach churning. I unlock the door, lean over, and empty my stomach next to the left front tire. I manage to get behind the wheel. Before I can start the car, I pass out.

I wake up to the sound of a key tapping on my car window. "Lady, are you alright?" a man asks in a concerned voice.

I realize my face is smashed against the steering wheel. I roll down the window and squeak out the words, "I'm not sure."

CHAPTER 20

I'm back home in my comfy chair trying to recover from my trip to the *Herald-Star*. Bridgette, Joe, and the twins drove to the newspaper parking lot to rescue me. Bridgette took me home and the twins gave me kisses where my face planted itself into the steering wheel. Joe drove my car and stopped to pick up pizzas so we could all eat dinner together.

I'm feeling better and create a new plan. I pick up my iPhone and call Juliette Mirow, the genealogist. I ask her to contact her connection in Sweden and gather as much information as she can on Carlton Bergstrom, who most likely left the US for Sweden in December 1959. I tell her he may have lived in Vasterbottens County where he had relatives.

"I'll get right on it," Juliette says.

"I don't want to tell you it's urgent, but it is really important to my elderly mother."

I hang up and go to the next call—Tim Konig.

"Mrs. Albrecht," Tim says in a sing-song voice. "I haven't heard from you in a while. What's up?"

"Tim, can you dig out the police report on my father's death from December 1, 1959? I found an article from the *Herald-Star* saying his body was discovered in the Rosewood apartment building and that he was last seen early that morning with his cousin Carlton Bergstrom. I know that Carlton disappeared after that. To my knowledge no one knows where he went, and I suspect he may have left the country. The murderer was never found."

"Oh, wow, Mrs. A," he says. "It may take me a couple days to search for a report that's 62 years old. But we have a warehouse with old records, so I'll tell my boss I need to find it. I'll tell him it's important."

"Thanks."

"By the way, you said your father's cousin's name is Carlton Bergstrom. What's your father's name?"

"Jefferson Arno Bergstrom Jr., born June 22, 1937."

• • •

I hit the wrong setting on my toaster when I put in a bagel. Now there's a smokey haze wafting through my kitchen—residuals from a bread product that now resembles a giant black O-ring.

I open my kitchen door to blow the smoke out, and a draft of January air cascades into my house. I pull my bathrobe tight and wave today's *Herald-Star* around the table to dissipate the smell. Silky trots into the kitchen and decides it's time to go outside. I wave her out and my phone rings. It's Tim.

"Hiya, Mrs. A, I've got news."

Tim tells me he found the police report from December 1, 1959, and a few other papers.

"Can you come at 2:00 p.m. today and we'll show them to you?" he says.

"I'll be there."

My Dodge Caravan is almost out of gas, and I need to fill the tank. It's so cold outside that I hate to stand at the gas pump, but it must be done—yet another reason I miss Anders. He took good care of my car.

I arrive right on time for my appointment with Tim at the police station. I anxiously sign in at a desk, and a female officer I've never met comes out to meet me.

"Follow me," she says matter-of-factly.

I go down the now-familiar hallway into the depth of the building. I'm led into a room with folders spread across a table. A paper map is push-pinned to a bulletin board. *How old-fashioned.*

"Have a seat, ma'am," the officer gestures with a petite hand. I notice her fingernails are painted with green polish. *Odd.*

I sit down, and five seconds later the door opens. I smile, expecting Tim. Instead, it's Sergeant Gambino. *Damn, damn, damn.*

"Mrs. Albrecht," he says with all the charm of Darth Vader. "Officer Konig has been called out on assignment, so you're stuck with me."

I smile weakly.

"We've found the police report and investigation notes from December 1959. Here's what we know. On the night your father died, he worked at your grandfather's cigar store into the early morning hours. He left and went to a place called Post-Time Recreation in the south end to meet up with some friends and his cousin Carlton. It seems Carlton frequented Post-Time because they had a fight club every Saturday night."

"Fight club?"

"Yes. Men would volunteer to fight each other. They'd draw for who would fight who, and patrons would bet on them. According to reports, Carlton was a tough guy. That night he drew another very good fighter. He happened to be the brother of the police chief. The two of them went at each other, and Carlton lost. Your father was seen escorting his cousin out. Some people reported they heard the two of them arguing in the parking lot."

"I see."

"Residents in the Rosewood building then heard noise in Apartment 2-D around 4:00 a.m. The manager of the building checked that apartment at 7:00 a.m. and found your father dead. Here's the toxicology report," he says, handing me a piece of paper. "It shows he ingested poison—strychnine. Someone wanted him dead. No one knows who else was in the apartment, but the person who rented the place during that time still lives in Steubenville."

"Who rented that apartment?"

"Charisse Duhamel."

• • •

I'm standing outside the door of Charisse's condo. I'm almost positive she is here because her car is in the parking lot. I want her to answer my questions. I knock.

"This is a nice surprise," Charisse says, holding a shot glass. "You caught me having a nip of Jack Daniels. Want some?"

"No thanks. I'm not here on a social call. I've seen the police report from December 1, 1959, and I've been out to Brimstone to see Chip Hanover," I say as calmly as I can. Now I'm coming to see you to ask what you know about the night my father died."

Charisse takes a deep sigh and starts by saying Carlton had a lively personality and deep passions. At times he could be moody. Other times he could be cocky. He had plans for his life but couldn't quite get them off the ground. He could get argumentative. Other times he was the life of the party, especially when he was drinking. Jefferson was more of a gentleman. He was polite and nicely dressed. He had a nice pocket watch and was always on time.

"One thing the two men had in common was the fact both were fascinated by gold and garnets," she explained. "I was already living in Rosewood Apartments when Jefferson first came to Steubenville in late 1958. He was doing some kind of business with Gino, even though he worked at Keystone Driller Company in Beaver Falls. Gracie and I first met Jefferson briefly in the cigar store. He told both of us to come up to Beaver Falls to go dancing at the Gold Mine. We did and we got to meet Carlton. He was known as the "blonde beatnik" because he loved poetry."

Charisse explained the two Bergstroms started coming to Steubenville every weekend to visit, and soon both couples started dating. By then Carlton had started working at Keystone too. Gracie was living at home with Gino and Viviana, and the two cousins would stay at Charisse's apartment most weekends.

"As you know," Charisse says, "Gracie and Jefferson ran off to Pittsburgh to get married in mid-June. They were quite in love, and Gracie was pregnant with you. Your grandparents were furious but calmed down enough to let your parents live with them for a month until they found an apartment. Then Gracie and Jeff moved to Brimstone in the triplex owned by the Hanovers."

Charisse stops for a second to blow her nose and compose herself. I brace myself for what's next.

"Gino was thinking about retiring and letting Jeff run the cigar store. Jeff seemed trustworthy—as much as is possible in Steubenville. The night of his death, I had driven out to Brimstone in late afternoon to stay all night with Gracie. She was eight months pregnant with you. I gave my apartment keys to Carlton so he and Jeff could sleep there after work, because the cigar store was open so late on Saturday nights.

"As I understand it, Jeff left the cigar store and met Carlton at a back-door joint on the south side in the Badlands. Carlton was supposed to fight a guy who happened to be the sheriff's brother. His name was Duke Maynard, and he was known around town as one nasty son of a bitch. I guess Jeff tried to get Carlton to leave, but he insisted on staying. Carlton got the snot knocked out of him. Then Jefferson jumped in and socked Duke in the jaw. I was told by an eyewitness that there was a lot of yelling as the Bergstroms left. Rumor was that Duke threatened to kill both Carlton and Jefferson."

"That's what it says in the police report," I confirm.

"Here's where everything gets fuzzy. I'm told they found your father's body in my living room. Whoever poisoned him obviously put something in his drink. Carlton had disappeared, but so had the sheriff's brother. No one saw either man leave the Rosewood, let alone what time each one left. Carlton was labeled as one of two suspects in your father's murder.

"At 7:30 the next morning I was washing dishes at Gracie's apartment when I saw Chip Hanover running down the lane towards us. I grabbed my bathrobe and went outside. He was hollering and waving his arms, yelling, 'Where's Gracie?' He reached the apartment and told us to get dressed and head to the hospital. The police would be waiting for us there."

I stand up and walk over to the window. "The report I saw today at the police station said the cause of death was strychnine poisoning in his drink."

"Yes," Charisse said. "I guess that's right. Gracie and I told the police everything we knew. The police contacted Pittsburgh, Youngstown, Cleveland, and Beaver Falls to search for Carlton. They never found him, and we never heard from him again. Gracie said she didn't know his family, so she couldn't contact them."

"That is so sad," I sigh.

"One more thing, Mo. The police thoroughly searched both my Rosewood apartment and Gracie's Brimstone apartment. They told us some of Jefferson's personal effects were missing. One of the missing items was his pocket watch."

"Such a shame," I say. "I would love to have it."

"I know," Charisse replied. "I dated a policeman once who told me sometimes killers like to take souvenirs from their victim's body."

I thank Charisse and get ready to leave.

"Wait a minute, honey," she says. "I have two pictures to give you."

She roots around in her desk and pulls out two black-and-white photos marked *Kisco* on the back. Kisco was a large printing plant for family photos during the 1950s. "I took this one of your mom and dad, and then Gracie snapped this one of Carlton and me. You can see both cousins were handsome. Carlton had beautiful blonde curls on the top of his head, but he also had a bad scar above his right eye. I'm guessing it was due to his love for fighting."

CHAPTER 21

I'm driving to Mingo Junction to check on Gracie's house. I approach a business with a sign board that says *Safe-T-Salt on Sale Today*. The sidewalks are icy this time of year, and I can use some salt at my house. I pull in.

The business is Hayney's Feed & Farm Supply, which has been there for 60 years. The Hayneys' daughter, Jolene, was my BFF through high school. We spent hours during those teenage years telling each other all our greatest secrets. It all seems so silly now.

I head inside, and low and behold there is Jolene behind the counter. She sees me and runs out for a hug. "So good to see you!"

Jolene tells me her son runs the store and she helps now and again. "It happens my mom is in the back room today."

We chat, and I tell her I finally have a picture of my father. "I'm still trying to track down his killer. It could be his cousin. I just got a photo of both men. I found out yesterday my dad died by strychnine poisoning."

Suddenly, I hear "Whose voice is that?" from the back room. "Oh my! Is it Mo?"

"Yes, Mom. Come out here."

Mrs. Hayney appears and gives me a hug. "Why are you talking about strychnine, of all things?"

"The police told me that's how my dad died—strychnine in his whiskey."

"That whole thing was terrible. I remember it like yesterday," Mrs. Hayney says. "Back in the day, I often attended Mass with Gracie. We were neighbors. That murder shook me up. Strychnine is nasty stuff—we used to sell it here. We sold quite a bit of it, in fact. The farmers would use it to kill rats, gophers, and coyotes. We stored it in a hidden room out back so no one could touch it."

"At least I now have a photo of my father and his cousin," I say. "Charisse Duhamel gave them to me yesterday."

"Let me see them," Mrs. Hayney says.

I hand her the photo, and she studies the images. "Is the man with the scar your dad's cousin?"

"Yes."

"I think I remember him," she says. "I saw him in here twice. He was handsome with curly hair, but his hands looked rough. Funny how you don't forget people like that."

"Was he alone?" I ask.

"Yes."

"Are you willing to tell the police he was here?"

"I don't know why not. Maybe it would help you," she says. "It's terrible to grow up without a father."

• • •

I'm sitting in Gracie's empty living room with a notebook. Each time I get a new clue on my father's death I write it down. I also keep a list of phone numbers of everyone I talk to. I call it the Death Diary.

I've just added notes on my latest trip to see Sergeant Gambino and my encounter with Mrs. Hayney. I review everything starting with Gracie meeting Jefferson in late 1958 in Steubenville through the night of his death in 1959. *One year.*

I review everything I know about Jefferson's early life—his birth in North Creek and his schooling up until the time his parents moved to Glens Falls. Did he graduate from high school before joining the army or did he enlist because his parents couldn't support him? I know he was stationed at Fort Stewart, at least for a time. While there he met a musician friend connected with a jazz club in Harrisburg. He worked there a while then took a job in Beaver Falls at the Keystone Driller Company where he was joined by Carlton.

Of huge interest to me are the reasons for living in Harrisburg and Beaver Falls. There is a real mystery about searching for gold as well as an interest in garnets. I remember Gracie muttering about red ponies and Tim Konig explaining it was code for fencing stolen goods. There may be a connection.

I happen to have my iPad with me, and I start searching newspapers in the Glens Falls area as I have in the past. I focus on stories about Barton Mines and use the search engine to ferret out stories of stolen gems. I'm knee deep in the recesses of the Internet when I come upon a story from early 1958. The headline shouts *Thousands of Raw Garnets Stolen from Storage Area.*

Only five species of garnets are worth cutting and polishing—grossularite, spessartine, almandine, pyrope, and andradite. They all have the same crystalline structure, but their chemical composition is different. Jefferson and Carlton must have known these things. Were the Bergstrom cousins involved? Were they the red ponies?

I glance at my watch and realize I must get back to my house. Olivia has a piano recital, and I invited Charisse to come.

• • •

I'm sitting in a school auditorium waiting for the recital to begin. Charisse is happy to see Bridgette, Joe, and Max. Bridgette tells her that the pregnancy is going smoothly.

"I had only a little morning sickness with this pregnancy—not like the last time," Bridgette says. "I'm hoping I can work until the end of the school year."

The concert goes well, and Olivia shows real progress with her piece. I drive Charisse home, and as I pull into her parking lot she pulls two items out of her purse. They look like some sort of tools.

"I meant to give these to you this morning when you were here," she says. "Both of these things were left in my Rosewood apartment by Carlton. The police looked at them when they scoured my place for evidence of Jeff's murder. They didn't take them, so I stored them in the back of my sock drawer. I had forgotten about them until recently."

I pick up the tools and see one has a small but powerful magnifying glass and the other has a brush-type attachment.

"Strange," I say. "I have no idea what they are. I'll show them to Joe."

• • •

It's a Saturday, and Bridgette has asked me to come and take the kids for a few hours while she rests. Joe is working until late afternoon, so the house will be quiet. I ask the kids on the phone if they want to go see the latest Disney movie, and they get all excited.

"Ice cream after the movie?" Max asks.

"Sure. You know I'm a sucker for Rocky Road. *Mutto Bene.*"

The movie is cute and the kids stuff themselves with nachos and Starburst candy. We leave the theatre, and I fulfill my promise to stop for ice cream. We get to their house, and I see Joe is home. I grab the tools Charisse gave me and head inside.

"Joe, can you tell me what these are?" I ask. "Charisse had them. They were Carlton's."

He looks them over with concern. "This one is a jeweler's loupe, and the other is a Dremel. Both are tools used by gemologists in the making of jewelry. The loupe allows the jeweler to examine gems, and the Dremel is used to grind and polish them. Did you say they were Carlton's?"

"Yes. Charisse said the police examined them when searching her apartment after my father's death. They left them there without comment. I guess they were not important."

"Well, I'd hang onto them for now," Joe says. "Something tells me they are part of something nefarious."

• • •

Before I walk through the door of Gracie's room, I hear her talking as she lies in the bed. There is no one else in the room.

"Bee, I need you to make dinner for mother tonight," Gracie says. "Did you stop at the store today and pick up the mild Italian sausage?"

I stand where Gracie can see me. "I'm here, Mom."

"Bee?"

"No, it's me—Mo."

"Mo, where's Bee?"

It is at moments like this that I can either tell her the truth, which will upset her, or just go ahead and lie.

"She's working late at the library," I fib.

Gracie and Bee were born two years apart. Gracie was younger and had trouble pronouncing "Beatrice" so she became "Bee." Both young women showed promise in school, but scholarships in higher education were hard to come by in a blue-collar town like Steubenville.

Gino was able to pull enough money together to send Bee to Youngstown for one year of college. She missed her hometown after her freshman year, so Bee returned to "Little Chicago" and took a job in the library. She never married but found solace in reading and helping others discover the wonders of books. She also volunteered to work in the food pantry at church and seemed to be satisfied with her lot in life. At age 50, she developed lung cancer and died. Gino had passed away two years before her, so Gracie took care of Viviana.

Life had never been easy for Gino Rivers's family but they always managed to make do. Now here is Gracie, confined as a prisoner to failing health. Her active imagination is carrying her into a world that doesn't exist, but one in which she feels comfortable.

"Tell Mama I hope to not be late for supper," Gracie says to me. "I'll bring wine and garlic bread."

CHAPTER 22

I had a fitful night's sleep, and I don't know why. Silky got so disgusted with me that she uttered a harrumph in dog talk and left the room. It will soon be February, and so far the winter has been bad but not horrible. We've had worse. Yet I worry that Bridgette will fall on the ice or her kids will get hurt. She says I worry too much.

I go outside and put Safe-T-Salt on my sidewalk and head back inside with plans for a hot cup of tea and a good book. As I step back into my house, the phone rings.

"Maureen, this is Juliette Mirow. I've found out what happened to Carlton Bergstrom. My connection in Sweden did some detective work and found Carlton arrived into the Port of Stockholm on Christmas Day 1959," she explains. "His customs papers state his destination was Vasterbottens County. He took a job in one of the iron ore mines there and worked under the name C. Erik Bergstrom."

"Makes sense. His father's name was Erik," I say. "I'm guessing Erik is his middle name."

"After a few years he took a job in a beer distribution company, hauling kegs to taverns. My contact person searched through county records and could not find out if he ever married. She did find a police record stating he died on December 24, 1975."

"I see," I say.

"My contact searched through the local newspapers and found he died in a fight near a campground in the Umea Municipality. The place is called Kvarkenfisk. It's right on the Gulf of Bothnia across from Finland. The killer broke a bottle and cut his throat. He bled to death. The killer went to prison."

"Thanks, Juliette," I say. "You and your contacts have solved part of a big family mystery."

I hang up, go to the window, and stare at a large icicle hanging from the gutter. It is pointed straight down at me, and I take it as a sign. I need to go and tell Gracie about Carlton.

• • •

Gracie is sitting in the Broda chair half-asleep when I arrive at Silver Belles. The tray next to her bed has a snack-size bag of potato chips lying open with some of its contents spilled onto the floor. I notice an ant is trying to drag a piece of one under the bed.

I gently touch Gracie's arm. "Mom, it's Mo."

No response.

I turn off her TV so she can hear me better. I speak louder. She stirs slightly. I sit in silence for a while then try again. On the nightstand is a statue of the Blessed Virgin. A rosary lies next to it. The Christmas tree from two years ago is still in the corner. The paper Valentine is still taped to the wall. But something seems different—I can't explain it. The air is different. The shadows are different. Just different.

Gracie rallies a bit and looks directly at me. "You look pretty," she says.

"Thanks Mom. You seem sleepy today."

"I was dreaming about Papa. Is he here?"

"No, he's not."

"What about Jefferson?"

It's only the second time I've ever heard her say my father's name. "No, he's not," I say.

"Well, if he's not here, just have Carlton come and pick me up. I want to go home," Gracie says.

"He can't come, Mom."

"Why not? He said he would come and get me. I know he would do anything I ask."

"He can't come. He's dead. He died in a fight."

"Oh dear. Jeff said that it would happen to him someday. Sorry."

Sorry? Why would she say that?

I think about this all the way to my car. Once in the Caravan, I turn my thoughts to something much nicer—my noon luncheon date with my friend Jolene Hayney. It will give me a chance to relax.

• • •

Jolene and I are sitting in a cute café catching up with everything that's happened in our lives since Anders died. I put my phone in silent mode and toss it in my purse so we won't be disturbed. We laugh at ourselves sitting in an establishment in Steubenville's once notorious south end.

"Remember when our parents and grandparents warned us never to come here to the Badlands?" Jolene says. "It was a real hellhole in its early years. More murders per mile than any town in Ohio."

We take turns bragging about our grandkids, and I tell her Bridgette is expecting twins at age 40.

"Wow. I hope everything goes well," Jolene says. "There's nothing better in this life than helping with grandkids. I have six of them now."

Before we know it, we have been sitting there for two hours and we both need to leave. We make plans for a future lunch together and hop in our cars. I turn on my iPhone, and it lights up like the Fourth of July. There are five calls from Silver Belles and two from Bridgette. Something is wrong.

• • •

It is normally a 15-minute drive from the south end of Steubenville to Silver Belles. I am there in eight. As I run down the hall, I feel like my feet are stuck in cement. I reach my mother's doorway and absorb the sights and sounds of three people—Gracie mumbling softly in the bed, Bridgette weeping in a chair, and a priest giving voice to last rites. I freeze. Is this real?

When the priest is finished, the room is silent. A nurse appears after a moment and checks Gracie's pulse. "I'm sorry," she says, as she touches me on the shoulder and walks out.

The priest slips out of the room too. It's just Bridgette and me alone with Gracie's corpse. I try to make words come out of my mouth, but I fail.

• • •

People are standing in line to hug me at Gracie's calling hours. Friends I haven't seen since Anders's death and a few old neighbors have come to pay condolences. All the Hanover family stop by as well as the Hayneys. The retired teachers' association has sent flowers, and the principal from the high school where I taught says he hopes I can return to do some substitute teaching. I can't think about that now.

As the line of mourners begins to thin, Olivia and Max approach me. Both have something they want me to place in Gracie's casket. Max has made a tiny model airplane created from Legos, and Olivia has drawn a picture of a butterfly.

"Grandma Gracie will have these with her in heaven," I say.

"*Grazie.*"

• • •

We are sitting in the front row of St. Peter's Catholic Church. The priest is saying Mass. I'm so emotionally drained that I'm barely paying attention to his words. The pipe organ sounds wonderful, however, and it distracts me from the tension of the day. I glance up at the altar as I had so many times in my youth. Behind it is a beautiful painting of Christ, St. Peter, and Pope John Paul II. I'm suddenly smitten with the majesty of it all—something that has not happened to me since I was 13. Bridgette begins to poke me in the side, telling me to stand up. It's time to follow the casket down the aisle. Soon the hearse is loaded, and Bridgette and I get in to accompany the body.

There are only a few cars in our line for the drive to Mt. Calvary Cemetery. The ride will not take too long. It's cold but sunny. We're lucky the snow isn't flying around us. It's only one week until Ash Wednesday, but February in Ohio is always chilly this time of year.

We arrive at the cemetery, and Bridgette and I get out of the hearse. Joe and the twins are right behind us. Max takes my left hand and Olivia takes my right as we walk up the hill to the family plot. We all shiver as we take our place sitting on chairs set up for us next to the grave. Charisse is beside Joe.

"Grace Viviana Rivers." The priest is saying her name. It's the last time she will be above ground. She receives words of committal. It's over.

I show the twins Gino and Viviana's graves. To Viviana's right is Aunt Bee. Gracie is next to Bee. They are together in death—a family once again.

As we turn to leave, I spot a hawk circling the trees above the cemetery. A hawk's ability to maintain a steady course with its powerful wings is something I find fascinating. Almost every time I walk in Beatty Park, I see one or more hawks using their razor-sharp eyes to scope out the area.

I think about Gracie's mother-in-law, Eleanora Birdsong Bergstrom, and her forebears, who were Seneca. The hawk is a symbol of their tribe. *How ironic.*

The Native Americans had great reverence for the sky. It was where the knowledge of the four seasons and the calendar developed. Furthermore, the moon, stars, and comets held special powers and had powerful forces. The sky and the birds that flew there held a special place in their hearts.

Was this Eleanora's way of being part of Gracie's funeral? Two women who never met but who once shared a love for one man—Jefferson A. Bergstrom Jr.

CHAPTER 23

It's now March, and I've been able to get copies of Gracie's death certificate to open her estate. I had to call Bennington Southwick to ask who he could recommend as a probate attorney. He gave me the phone number of his nephew, Ellis Southwick. I know I can trust him. Now I need to get serious about selling Gracie's house. I need to hire an appraiser and get the place cleaned out. I can't have Bridgette help me with the last of my mother's household items because she needs to rest. I enlist Charisse. She can't carry and lift things, but she can keep me company.

We put the last items from Gracie's desk and vanity in boxes. Bridgette wants Joe to come and take the bed, desk, and dresser. They may need to buy a bigger house once the new twins arrive.

We move to the kitchen. I tell Charisse I will sell the refrigerator and stove with the house, as well as the washer and dryer in the basement. The dollhouse in the garage will be cleaned up and taken to Bridgette's house. Her doctor thinks one of the expectant twins is a boy, the other a girl. We sit at Gracie's small kitchen table that will be given to the Salvation Army donation center.

Gracie and I had thousands of meals sitting here—just the two of us. Her chair is now filled by Charisse.

"You'll be glad when the sale of this place is finally completed," Charisse says. "You'll be able to turn the page and proceed with your life. Your mom always seemed contented here—it was her safe space for the last 56 years."

"She did seem happy here," I say, "but I have to wonder why she was not interested in getting married again."

"In her own way Gracie may have been protecting you."

"But I wanted her to be happy. Instead, she occasionally seemed overly worried, almost anguished."

"All mothers worry."

"But this is different from the way I worried about Bridgette and Toby. And then the worst thing in the world happened to Toby. At least I had Anders to talk to. She was here all alone."

"I know. It was heartbreaking."

"Gracie's heart was broken twice—her husband's death and Toby's. But she never talked about Jefferson—it took until the very end for her to even say his name. And why, oh why, did she ask me to find Carlton? Why was that important?"

Charisse looks at me with a face I've never seen before. She grabs my hand. "Mo, I hope Gracie forgives me for telling you, but Carlton may be your biological father."

I'm flat out dumbstruck. The kitchen is spinning, so I grab the table with both hands. My mouth is gaping. It takes me two minutes to fully process this jolting revelation.

"How do you know that?" I ask.

"Your mother hinted this to me several times over the last 60 years. Gracie made me promise never to tell you. That's why in the last year she asked you several times to bring her rye toast with cheese. It was Carlton's favorite breakfast. Everything else about him she kept hidden."

"Now I'll never know for certain."

"There may be one way," Charisse explains. "Carlton had beautiful curly hair. One night it had gotten long and he asked me to trim a bit off the top until he could see a barber. After he left my apartment, I put a couple of his curls in an envelope. I admit, I really did love the guy. It was my way of keeping part of him no matter what happened between us. I still have the hair samples in my jewelry case."

"I can take that sample along with a clip of my hair and send it to a good DNA testing lab. It may or may not be definitive."

"If you decide to do it, I'll support you. But it's a big step."

• • •

I've been to the post office to mail my DNA samples and I'm headed out to Mingo Junction to meet with the real estate agent. I pass Hayney's Feed & Supply but don't have time to stop and see if Jolene is there. She and her mother came to Gracie's funeral, and we've made plans to have lunch again in two weeks.

I pull into Gracie's driveway and see the agent's car in front of the house. Her name is Emily and she's a cousin of Joe's. I wave to her and motion towards the front door.

We go inside and sit at Gracie's kitchen table to sign the contract to sell the house. I tell her I have an appraisal and that Gracie's estate has been set up with the probate court, so I'm free to go ahead.

"I know it's hard to sell your childhood home," Emily says. "I'll do my best to make it as smooth as possible. The end of winter is not necessarily the best time to sell a house, but soon it will be spring. Hope always blooms in the spring."

She leaves, and I walk through the house to check on a few things. Joe has already picked up Gracie's bedroom furniture. I go through the kitchen cupboards again and find a coffee cup tucked back in a corner that I gave Gracie for Christmas my senior year of high school. It says, *World's Greatest Mom*.

I lock the front door and leave through the back. As I pull out of the driveway, I see the *For Sale* sign for the first time in the front yard. Again, it jolts my heart. I can't wait for this chapter of my life to close. It's almost Easter, and after that will come spring—*Primavera* in Italian. *Always hope.*

• • •

It's Easter morning, and I'm at Bridgette's house, cooking brunch while they are at Mass. Once they return, I want Bridgette to go rest and we'll eat at 2:00 p.m. Bridgette is still feeling well, but of course she tires easily.

The day goes smoothly. We're lucky with Easter being April 9 this year that the weather has held sunny at 59 degrees. Joe and I finish the dishes, and there are a couple hours of daylight left. I tell them that I'm going to drive out to Mt. Calvary Cemetery to put a flower on Gracie's grave. Olivia wants to go with me. Bridgette goes off to rest again while Joe and Max play video games.

As I drive to the cemetery, I play a CD of Bach's *Mass in B minor* for Olivia to hear.

"Bach was old and blind when he wrote this," I tell her. "It is an amazing piece. If you stick with your music lessons, someday you will be able to play this in an orchestra."

My car is not the only one parked in the cemetery today. I spot families and individuals still in their church clothes standing near graves. Olivia takes it all in and asks particularly good questions. She is a bright child, and soon she will be helping her mother with twin siblings. She has no idea how her life is going to change.

We park the car near the Rivers family plot, and she grabs my hand. I let Olivia place the flowers on the grave.

"Can Grandma Gracie see us?" she asks.

"She's right with us," I say. "We will always carry her in our hearts."

"Mommy said that Great-Grandma Gracie never told us the whole story of her life. Will you promise me that you will tell me yours when I get bigger?"

"I swear."

"Pinkie swear?" Olivia pleads.

I extend my hand and hook my little finger around hers. "Pinkie swear, always."

I brought along a blanket in case we wanted to sit for a while before the sun sets. Olivia loves the idea. She likes to learn about nature, so we talk about the trees, the sky, and the birds. Just before we're ready to leave, a butterfly floats past us and lands on top of Gracie's gravestone. Olivia smiles a smile I've seen many times on Bridgette's face.

"Butterflies," Olivia smiles. "New life."

. . .

I've had one of the best night's sleep I've had since Gracie first got sick. I make strong tea and try to get the cobwebs out of my head. I plan to spend the day nestled together with an enjoyable book.

My phone rings. It's the bank manager from Gracie's bank where she and I have a joint account. "Your mother has a safe deposit box here, and I wonder if she's going to renew it?"

"Gracie died a couple weeks ago, and I'm her executor," I reply. "The estate has been set up so, I can come and clean out the box. I didn't know she had one—she never mentioned it. I don't even have the key."

"We'll let you in. If you think there's items in it, bring a box."

I know an inventory list of everything in the box will need to be filed with the estate. I will contact Ellis Southwick to accompany me to the bank. I want everything to be done correctly. Will there be any surprises in the box? I have a feeling my life is about to change again.

CHAPTER 24

I'm heading into Gracie's bank to clean out her safe deposit box and meet up with my lawyer, Ellis Southwick. First we're ushered into an office, and I explain I don't want to retain Gracie's box and need to close it out. I sign some paperwork, and the bank officer hands me a key and leads us inside the bank vault.

"Just close the door when you both are finished," she says flatly.

A pull on the lid brings more revelations of Gracie's hidden past. There is a bag with more garnets in it, a few more gold coins, and some savings bonds with my maiden name on them. I grab a folded piece of yellowing paper and see that it is my father's death certificate from the Jefferson County Department of Vital Statistics. It states his place of birth as North Creek, New York. Cause of death—poisoning. He was 23 years old.

The next item is a small box. A lovely piece of artwork—an alabaster eagle about the size of a large egg—sits nestled in a fluffy cotton bed. It is accompanied by a handwritten note.

> *Dear Gracie, I'm thrilled to hear of the birth of Jefferson's daughter. When you think the time is right, please give this to her. I'm told she has a pretty name—Maureen Grace. All My Best, Eleanora.*

An alabaster eagle sent from my paternal grandmother just for me! Why did Gracie hide it? Did she ever send a message back to Eleanora?

The next items are two connected black-and-white photos, the kind that come in a strip of three from an amusement park photo booth. Obviously one photo has been cut off. There is a young couple laughing. The woman is my mother, but I don't know the man, or do I? I look closer. The man has curly hair—it must be Carlton!

There's one more item at the bottom of the box—an envelope. The postmark is dated December 7, 1959, from New York City and addressed to Gracie Bergstrom, c/o Chip Hanover, Route 151, Mingo Junction, Ohio. There is no return address, and the envelope does not look like it has ever been opened. Yet it must be important for Gracie to have kept it for 62 years. Who did she know in New York City? Why didn't she open it?

Ellis has me sign the inventory so he can file it with the probate court. I put everything in the box, shut the door, and leave. As I drive home I think about what I'm going to do with all the garnets and gold coins in Gracie's estate. When I reach home I put the box on my kitchen table, feed Silky, and decide to see what's in the mystery correspondence.

> *Dearest Gracie, I'm sending this to you in care of Chip because I can't remember your exact address in*

> the triplex. I'm certain the post office will find the Hanovers and deliver it to you. I'm in New York City and will be leaving soon. I've booked passage on the Swedish American Line to Stockholm. I should be there by Christmas. It's not steerage but I'm not hiding in the boiler room either. Take good care of the baby. I know you will. I will cherish the little photo of us that you gave me and keep it in my wallet forever. C.

I'm thunderstruck. There's no doubt in my mind that this is Carlton's handwriting. The letter proves he was running away. I see no evidence that Gracie ever opened this correspondence. Why not? I wonder if Gracie ever heard from him again. I take three deep breaths and decide to do something I thought I would never, ever do. I dial the police station and ask to speak to Sergeant Gambino.

"Well, well, well, Mrs. Albrecht," Gambino says, answering my call. "Of all people, I didn't think I would be hearing directly from you."

"My mother passed away a few weeks ago, and I've been going through her personal effects. I have uncovered some information that I think may pertain to my father's death. I realize it has been 62 years, but I've been told the case is considered unsolved. I'd like an opportunity to clear up a few things."

"That would be most interesting," Gambino says wryly. "Whatever you have must be clear-cut or it's not worth much. Can you give me an example of what you've found?"

"I can give you two. One has to do with Chip Hanover's father and his illegal moonshine operation. The second one involves the fight club Carlton Bergstrom belonged to and the fact he fought with the former police chief's brother in the Badlands the night my father died."

"How soon can you come in?"

• • •

The police department is being exceptionally courteous to me today. One officer spots me as I drive to the back of the station where Sergeant Gambino told me to park. The female police officer with the green nail polish (now replaced by ruby red) greets me and makes a motion to follow her. Instead of going into a stark interrogation room with dull beige walls and grey metal chairs, I'm taken to an office with a draped window, plush chairs, and a coffee pot.

"Care for a cup of Joe?" the officer asks. "It's premium stuff—donated by the market next door."

I shake my head and she disappears. Soon Sergeant Gambino enters. Along with spotless new shoes, he seems to have been retrofitted with a more pleasant personality.

"So, you've been doing some detective work, eh?"

"I may be able to add some clarity to Jefferson Bergstrom's death," I say. "I've come across possible new evidence since my mother died."

"Okay, so lay the cards on the table."

"I'll start with the red ponies. My mother talked about them—the fencers. As much as I hate to admit it, I feel certain my father and his cousin delivered stolen goods to Steubenville from Gore Mountain. I talked to Chip Hanover, and he showed me where his father hid moonshine for the locals. He also let other men hide goods there. Among his clients were the Bergstroms."

"Any proof of that?" Gambino asks bluntly.

"Here are a couple articles from the North Creek and Glens Falls newspapers describing the heist dated from 1959. I also have something else."

I dig into my purse and pull out two bags of garnets. "This bag was found yesterday in Gracie's safe deposit box, and this one was found recently in Chip Hanover's barn in a hidden underground compartment. The gems look very much alike. I'm sure experts could trace them."

"Is that all?"

"Oh no, there's plenty more."

I carefully explain that my mother met Jefferson at Big G's Cigar Store in late 1958 while he was working in Beaver Falls at Keystone Drilling Company. At times he would come to Steubenville to visit Grandpa Gino. Carlton visited Jefferson in Beaver Falls and decided to take a job there too. Soon both men were coming to Steubenville, and Carlton started dating Charisse Duhamel.

I explain that after my parents were married they moved to the triplex in the Brimstone area. Jefferson was working for Gino.

"On the night he died, Charisse stayed all night with Gracie in Brimstone," I explain. "Charisse also gave my father the key to her apartment so he didn't have to drive out there at 4:00 a.m. You well know from the police report that the former sheriff's brother, Duke Maynard, and Carlton fought each other that night. Carlton lost, and Jefferson turned around and clobbered Duke upside the head. Charisse said an eyewitness overheard Duke say he'd kill both men.

"Jefferson took his cousin back to Charisse's apartment to patch him up. Someone heard a commotion in the apartment about 4:00 a.m. The police report said they found three whiskey glasses and a bottle of Jack Daniels on the living room coffee table. The fingerprints had been wiped off the glasses. Obviously either Duke or Carlton poisoned my father's whiskey. By morning Carlton had left town and my father was dead. Another person disappeared that night too—Duke Maynard."

"Anything else?"

"You bet there is. It seems Carlton made his way from Steubenville to New York City, where he booked passage on the Swedish American Line. He arrived around Christmas 1959 and headed up to a city called Robertsfors in Vasterbotten County, Sweden."

"How do you know that?"

"Just yesterday I found this letter from Carlton to my mother," I say, pulling an envelope from my purse. "It was written right before he boarded the ship to Sweden. You can see what it says. Again, Charisse has confirmed the handwriting. I also discovered a picture of my mother and Carlton together. He wanted Gracie to know that he's safe. He also hoped that the baby—me—would be well cared for."

"Why would he care," Gambino says. "He ran away and was taking a big chance by mailing this letter to Steubenville."

"He loved her and Gracie loved him," I reply.

"Did your mother confess that?"

"No, Charisse said she did. Gracie told her several times never to tell me. Charisse saved a sample of Carlton's hair, and I have sent it to a DNA testing lab to see if it matches mine."

"Is Carlton Bergstrom still alive?"

"No, he died in a fight in 1975. Someone cut his throat in a fishing village called Kvarkenfisk. He is buried in a Robertsfors cemetery."

"It still doesn't solve the poisoning."

"I have something on that too."

I explain that I visited Hayney's Feed & Seed and happened to see Mrs. Hayney. She and Gracie were friends. I showed her the photo of Carlton that Charisse gave me. Mrs. Hayney said Carlton was in her store twice. The second time he was alone and purchased strychnine. "Why would he need it? He was not a farmer and he didn't own land. I think he was up to something nefarious."

Gambino rocked back in his chair and rubbed the bottom of his chin for a moment. Then he sat up straight and leaned in towards me. "I'll take this to the prosecutor," he says. "They will make the decision on whether to close this case."

"Thanks."

"This is your family, Mrs. Albrecht, and your mother has passed," he says bluntly. "Wouldn't you rather just let this remain buried?"

"Too much has been kept hidden in this town. In my grandchildren's passage through life, I want them to witness honest people trying their best to live good lives."

CHAPTER 25

It's time once again for the annual Dean Martin Festival, but I won't be attending the Rat Pack Parade this year. I'm on a very special trip—one I could never have imagined a year ago. I'm driving east on I-76 to visit my cousin Sonja Lunden in Greensburg, where we will depart for Glens Falls, New York, to meet her mother, Maja. From there we will drive up to New Sweden, Maine, in time to catch the June Midsommar Festival.

To make this trip even more delightful, Bridgette and Joe are driving their recreational vehicle behind me to spend two nights camping in a Greensburg area RV park. Max and Olivia and their new twin siblings—who their parents lovingly named Grace Maureen and Joseph Jefferson—are with them.

Charisse is riding with me to Greensburg but will stay in a motel and assist Bridgette with the new babies. Charisse will ride back to Steubenville with Bridgette in the RV while I head to Glens Falls with my cousin Sonja. I will temporarily leave my car with Charisse so she can spend a few hours in the local casino, and I'll pick it back up once I return to Greensburg. With luck, it will all work out.

I arrive in Greensburg and head to Sonja's house. Joe and Bridgette are right behind. Both vehicles pull into Sonja's driveway. She hears the commotion and comes out to greet us. She is delighted to meet all the new relatives, especially the kids.

Sonja's husband is at a conference at Penn State University, so Sonja has prepared a late lunch for everyone before Joe and Bridgette head to the campgrounds and Charisse takes my car to the Holiday Inn Express. They will all meet up tomorrow to go camping while Sonja and I head together to Glens Falls. I must pinch myself to believe this is all real and not just a dream.

• • •

Sonja is maneuvering her car onto the I-99 freeway as we head northeast across the Keystone State. Ironically, the route will take us right past the city of State College, where Penn State University is located along I-80. Sonja jokes that she will wave to her husband as we drive by. We venture up into upstate New York, and I explain the complicated history of Steubenville and its history of illegal gambling operations connected to the Mafia kingpins from Cleveland, Youngstown, and Pittsburgh. I tell her gambling habits are a way of life for some people like Charisse—she dearly loves the adrenaline rush and the thrill of the risk.

"I'm not surprised," Sonja says. "I've read the *Pittsburgh Gazette* since I was a child. They used to run all kinds of stories in the newspapers about the Cosa Nostra. I don't see those stories anymore, and the Greensburg area casino seems to do a decent job providing entertainment without Mafia ties. At least that's what it seems to me. I'm not a gambler," she laughs. "My husband and I hate to part with our money in games of chance. We don't have the desire or instinct."

I explain that my mother's side of the family are all Italians from the Calabria region. "My grandmother's parents and my grandmother emigrated to America from Naples. My grandmother, Viviana Marie Tattini, was three years old. My grandfather's parents were also from Calabria. Their surname was Flusso, but it was changed to Rivers at Ellis Island. At first, Gino's father worked in a saloon along the Ohio River, but eventually he went to work in the local steel mill. Grandpa Gino was born in Steubenville in 1913."

"Where exactly is the Calabria area?" Sonja asks.

"Calabria is the toe of the Italian boot. It is separated from Sicily by the Strait of Messina. My grandmother used to say Calabria was the safecracker capital of the world. Apparently it has quite a reputation."

"Your grandmother has a very pretty name," Sonja says.

"She was a lovely hardworking lady and quite religious. She owned a stationery store around the corner from my grandfather's cigar store. They were quite old school. Their families were living the American dream, even in a gritty town like Steubenville."

I make sure not to mention anything about gambling. I don't want the Bergstrom family members to get the wrong idea about me. I dearly want to get to know them better.

"So, you never knew your father. Is that correct?"

"Right, that's why I am so grateful that we have connected," I say. "I can't tell you what that means to me."

There is a lull in the conversation as Sonja maneuvers the car through a tricky bit of traffic. It gives me a moment to contemplate whether I should be frank about my Grandpa Gino's business dealings and my father's brief time working with him. Is it dishonest to hide the truth from my newly found relatives? At some point should I tell them? Will they think less of me? I've spent my whole life hoping I could find a connection with my father. I'm on the edge of opening a new door. Will that door close if I tell them what I have recently learned about Jefferson Bergstrom Jr. and his cousin Carlton? I try to break the tension in my head and accidentally emit a loud cough.

"Are you okay?" Sonja asks.

"I'm fine," I say. "I was just thinking about how lucky I am to be meeting Bergstrom family members."

Soon we are pulling into the driveway of Sonja's brother Fred. He's happy to see me again.

"Tomorrow we are going to have breakfast with Mother," he says. "Then we are all going to visit the grave of your paternal grandparents Jefferson and Eleanora Bergstrom."

"I can't wait to meet Maja—a relative who spent time with my very own father and grandfather! I know I won't sleep well. This is so exciting."

• • •

Fred drives Sonja and me across Glens Falls towards Maja's condo. He takes us past Poopie's Diner, which is not far from our destination.

"There it is," Fred declares. "You asked about it. If there is time after we return from the Midsommar Festival, we'll go there. I'm certain your grandparents ate in that place. It's still popular."

Five minutes later we arrive at Maja's condo. She hugs me tightly and tears of joy run down her face. "I'm so very happy to meet you," she beams.

Maja puts on a pot of tea and hauls out some Swedish cookies she has baked. "My grandmother brought this recipe from Sweden," she says. "I want you to feel right at home."

"Do you have memories of your grandmother?" I ask since I'm not certain of when she died and Maja's age at the time.

"I was named after my grandmother. Her maiden name was Annika Maja Lindholm, and she died when I was two years old, in 1943. My mother, Astrid, said her mother worried herself to death. My grandmother's brother, Karl Lindholm, was in the Swedish Resistance during World War II. As a history teacher, you know that Sweden was one of the few European countries to stay neutral. But you probably don't know that the Swedes sold iron ore to Germany during the war and the Krauts owned several mines near my grandmother's hometown. Karl Lindholm gave intelligence to the Allies and secretly helped to train refugees from Denmark and Norway to liberate their countries. They hated the Nazis. The war was a horrible time—even for a neutral country. You can't be neutral about something as awful as fascism."

"That's fascinating," I say. "I had no idea about the Lindholms."

"I have plenty of stories for you," Maja says. "Some of them involve illegal activities. Karl Lindholm came to Glens Falls to visit in the 1950s. Your father happened to be on leave from the army and was able to visit with him. They got along great—kindred souls, it seemed. I remember Karl told us he stole handguns from the Nazis. I believe he gave one to your father."

"Do you happen to know if the handgun was a Glock?" I ask.

"I don't know much about guns, but I'm certain it was a Glock. I was a teenager at the time, and I was shocked at the sight of it. But I picked it up and took a good look at it. I remember your father was excited to have it."

"I'm all ears."

• • •

Spending time in graveyards has become a new habit of mine, and I find myself in Glens Falls Cemetery. Near the entrance is a beautiful stone chapel with a slate roof. A sign says the cemetery is on the National Register of Historic Places. Maja, Fred, and Sonja are striding two by two among the stones. How fortunate I am to have them take me to my paternal grandparents' grave. Maja balances herself on Fred's arm to keep from falling. Soon we are staring at the double headstone of Jefferson Bergstrom Sr. and Eleanora Birdsong Bergstrom. There is a tiny symbol carved next to my grandfather's name.

"What is that?" I ask.

"It's called a Trinity Knot or a triquetra," Maja replies. "It originated in North Wales, but some of the Swedes adopted it. It's formed by three triangular Celtic knots, called triskeles, synonymous with interconnectedness. The fusion of three triskeles represents virtues such as faith, hope, and love. The symbol has been found in Norse Viking imagery on things like combs and saddles."

"And Eleanora has a hawk next to her name," I say. "I've been studying about the Seneca and their symbols. What an interesting married couple. I so wish I could have known them."

"Your grandfather was quite ill when I knew him, so I can't say much. But your grandmother had a sweet soul. She was very in tune with nature—very sensitive. After you've been to New Sweden for Midsommar Fest, we'll get back together and talk," Maja says. "There are many things you don't know."

I can only guess.

CHAPTER 26

I have never been to Maine before, and its beauty has surpassed all my expectations. The rocky coastline is commanding. I look out at the Atlantic, and my mind pictures wooden ships that found their way here in the seventeenth and eighteenth centuries sailing from New France (Canada) and Europe. How surprised they must have felt gazing at its craggy grandeur.

We are driving through Cape Elizabeth, which is part of the Portland Metro area. Fred tells me that Maine has 3,500 miles of tidal coastline (including islands)—more than California. I had never seen a lighthouse, and now I long to bring Bridgette's family up to Maine to see one.

"There's so much history in this place, Mo," Fred says. "In 1776, the people of Cape Elizabeth posted eight soldiers here to warn citizens of British attacks," he says. "George Washington ordered construction of the Portland Head Light, as they called it, at Cape Elizabeth. Interesting fact, Henry Wadsworth Longfellow was born in Portland. His poem "The Lighthouse" was probably based on the Portland Head Light."

We stop and eat lobster rolls in a little seafood shanty near the Cape. Fred continues to chat a blue streak, entertaining us with odd facts about the state. "It's the only state in the US that borders only one other state," he babbles with great flair. "It produces 90% of all our nation's toothpicks. Maybe it has something to do with the fact four-fifths of the state's land is under forest cover."

As we walk up to the cash register to pay the bill, Sonja spots a framed photo of a white pine cone. "Isn't that the symbol of the state?" she asks.

"Yep," Fred replies. "It's the state flower."

"Flower?" I ask. "I didn't know a pine cone is considered a flower."

"Up here it is," he laughs. "It's not actually a flower. It's the largest conifer in North America. But lawmakers picked it anyway because the white pine is the state's official tree."

"He's just full of fun facts," I laugh as we get in the car.

"That's not all he's full of," Sonja jokes.

We leave the Portland area and head inland towards Aroostook County and our destination of the New Sweden-Stockholm area. Three hours later we start to see billboards and signs for Aroostook State Park and Presque Isle. I can hardly contain my excitement. Somewhere in the deep recesses of my body, the Italian genes are being pushed aside and my Swedish genes are tingling. Once we get to New Sweden, we will be only a few miles from the Canadian border and, just beyond that, the St. Lawrence River.

• • •

We are singing the first stanza of a hymn by composer Marty Haugen called "All Are Welcome" while seated in the pews of Gustaf Adolph Lutheran Church in New Sweden. I must pinch myself when I realize my cousins and I are worshiping in the very church where my grandfather and his twin siblings were baptized. As the parishioners sing and smile at their guests, my mind wanders back to all the activities that have occurred over the last two days here. It has been a hectic 48 hours—all of which is playing like a newsreel in my brain accompanied by the melody of organ music.

We arrived in New Sweden on Friday afternoon in time to settle into a bed and breakfast and head out to the Swedish meatball supper at the American Legion Hall in Stockholm. After a good night's sleep, we attended the Midsommar Frukost (breakfast) at the Thomas Park Dining Hall before gathering for the raising of the Majstang (Maypole). We watched in awe as dancers of all ages performed ring dances to traditional Swedish music. Women and girls were dressed in costumes representing every part of Sweden—each one wearing a beautiful flower ring in her hair and an apron around her waist. Meanwhile the men and boys in knickers and vests clapped and danced with great vigor.

We walked the aisles of artisan booths selling handmade jewelry and art, then made our way to the New Sweden Historical Museum to look at their collection. We had only been there for ten minutes when Sonja spotted a local genealogist inviting visitors over to her table. She introduces herself as Annika.

"We wonder if you can find our grandparents?" Fred asked. "My grandmother, Astrid Bergstrom, and my cousin's grandfather, Jefferson Bergstrom, were born here." We give her the dates of their births which she puts into the name bank of her laptop's search engine. Within minutes we had an answer.

"Yes," Annika said. "They were baptized at the Lutheran church on Capitol Hill Road. The parents are listed as Nils Fredrik Bergstrom and Annika Maja Lindholm Bergstrom. The church has a book of records with all the baptisms, confirmations, and weddings listed in it. Some of it is written in Swedish. I'm a member there. We could be cousins."

"What a coincidence," Sonja said. "You have the same first name—Annika—as my great-grandmother. We know both her parents were born in Vasterbottens County, Sweden."

"Mine too!" Annika jumps up and gives us each a hug. "Let me tell you that the congregation has a big supper later this afternoon from 4:00-6:00 p.m. I'll be heading over there about 5 o'clock. Please come and join us. I'll introduce you to people."

It took only a few seconds for Fred, Sonja, and I to agree to meet Annika for supper. At the appointed time, Fred pulled the car into the church lot and we entered a scene right out of a Turner classic movie. Many of those seated at long tables were still in their costumes. A fiddler and an accordion player were seated in a corner, happily creating toe-tapping tunes. Some people were clapping along with the beat. Giggling children skipped in circles.

Annika introduced us to members of her congregation as if she had known us her whole life. One of the men whispered to Fred that if he wanted a shot of liquor called Aquavit all he had to do was meet him outside next to his car.

"We consider Aquavit to be the national drink of Sweden," the man said. "God doesn't want us to drink it in His house, but he doesn't care if we partake outside."

Once we had eaten a meal of salmon and herring, Annika took us to the church office and showed us the official book of records. She leafed through the pages until she came to a list from 1915. There in beautiful handwriting was the name Jefferson Arno Bergstrom, baptized on March 7, 1915. Two more pages were flipped, and the names Astrid Lovisa Bergstrom and Erik Nils Bergstrom (twins) appeared with the baptismal date June 22, 1918.

• • •

Now here I sit in the church of my Swedish great-grandparents in their adopted country. I wonder what the settlers thought of it once they had moved here. Were they terribly homesick or were they happy? A member of the congregation reads two Bible passages. The pastor reads the gospel lesson and delivers the sermon. I hear about Jesus's unconditional love and the word *grace* explained several times. I have heard that about Lutherans—it's all about grace. Lovely.

The closing hymn comes, and a robed acolyte is snuffing out the candles on the altar. Church bells are ringing to end the service. "Care for a cup of coffee?" Annika asks as some parishioners leave and others gather in the back of the building. "Some of the folks will want to greet you."

We grab our coffee and sit down to enjoy another dollop of church hospitality. An elderly gentleman leaning heavily on a cane approaches and says that he heard we were from Ohio.

"I am from Steubenville," I say, "and my cousin Fred here is from Glens Falls, New York, and his sister, Sonja, is from Greensburg, Pennsylvania."

"And you are all Bergstroms?" he asks, rubbing his chin.

"Yes!" I answer.

"My name is Herbert, and my father knew Erik Bergstrom. They graduated from school together before Erik moved away. They wrote Christmas cards to one another each year, then Erik died in the '70s. But I remember my dad said Erik had a son and a nephew who moved to Steubenville."

"That's right," I exclaim, amazed at the man's memory and the connection.

"My dad said there was trouble down there and one of them died by poisoning and the other one disappeared. Rumor was one of the two escaped to Sweden."

I take a big gulp and tried to harness the jitters now jetting through my body.

"The man who died was my father, Jefferson Jr., and the other was his cousin Carlton Bergstrom. Yes, I understand that he disappeared. I never knew my father, and my mother would not talk about either one of them."

I can see Fred and Sonja draw back in horror.

"That's too bad," Herbert says, frowning. "The word somehow made its way all the way up here to New Sweden in 1960. Unfortunately, there was a member of our congregation here at Gustaf Adolph Lutheran who might have used it as a model for poisoning members of our congregation in 2003. It made news all over the country."

"How so?" Fred asked, leaning deeply into the conversation.

Herbert asks if he can sit down with us, and we gladly offer him a chair. Herbert begins by saying the man who poisoned 16 church members in New Sweden was a loner who was angry at the world.

"The suspect in the case came here to church but did not listen to Christ's loving words," Herbert explains. "He slipped arsenic in the coffee pot one Sunday when no one was looking. The people who drank the coffee got sick and were rushed to the hospital in Caribou, thinking it was food poisoning. The police sent the coffee to the Maine CDC, where they discovered arsenic. The sickest of our members were quickly taken to Eastern Maine Medical Center, where one died. The suspect killed himself five days later. He left a suicide note. It was the largest mass poisoning in the US in modern history.

"It is quite a coincidence that the Bergstrom poisoning might have a tie to the poisoning here. One of our parishioners told us his father knew the story and talked about it to friends in 1960. It seems that one parishioner was a fan of Dean Martin and remembered reading a small story in the *Bangor Daily News* about a poisoning death in Ohio. The man recognized the place, Steubenville, and the name Bergstrom. He suspected it was Erik's son. His group of friends discussed it at length. Maybe the suspect in our poisoning case overheard them as a young man and remembered it. Later in life he took out his woes on our congregation in some weird act of revenge. I think he had some mental problems. You know, three Dalmatians short of a fire truck."

Fred, Sonja, and I stare at each other in utter amazement.

"We stopped serving coffee for a while," Herbert says. "But we are Lutherans and we love our coffee."

We say our goodbyes and thanks to Herbert and Annika as we head to the parking lot to leave New Sweden. I climb back into Fred's car with a heavy heart. A family tragedy I hadn't been able to explain yet has now been exposed to my cousins. It's going to be a long ride back to Glens Falls and a painfully long talk with Maja.

CHAPTER 27

I'm sitting in Poopie's Diner across from Maja Lunden. Sonja is seated next to her mother, and Fred is across from his sister. Until two days ago, I had been excited to hold this meeting with my three Bergstrom relatives. Instead, I feel defensive and deflated. The experience at the Gustaf Adolf Lutheran Church has left me shaken. What are the chances we would meet someone with information on Erik? Only in New Sweden could we have randomly met Herbert.

All along the drive from New Sweden back to Glens Falls, my thoughts were consumed with Carlton and how he might have been a role model for another man to poison people. Not only did one man die right away but Herbert said six others of those affected have died of various diseases in the last 20 years. Obviously, the poisoning weakened their bodies.

"Maureen," Maja says gently, "don't be embarrassed that you hadn't discussed the circumstances of your father's death with us yet. You haven't known us very long. I've been waiting to tell you what little I know about the circumstances surrounding your birth."

"I didn't feel I could talk to you on the phone about all this," I say, stuffing my shaky hands under the table so they can't be seen. "But there are so many unanswered questions."

Maja tells me that she only saw Jefferson twice when he came to visit his parents. She confirmed my father had already joined the army when my grandparents moved to Glens Falls, and she had never been to North Creek.

"Jefferson Jr. was handsome in his uniform," Maja recalls. "But he was rather mysterious. I remember he wore a garnet ring with little diamonds on either side. I thought it looked out of place on the hands of a soldier."

The garnet ring—so it was my father's!

"My mother, his Aunt Astrid," Maja continues, "talked to him about how Eleanora was handling her household but needed help with certain things. I was sent several times to watch over your grandfather when Eleanora had to leave the house. Mostly it was my mother who helped."

Maja explained her mother rarely heard from her twin brother Erik. He divorced and moved to Pennsylvania at some point. His son, Carlton, was with him for a while.

"The next thing mom hears is that Carlton and Jefferson Jr. are living together in Beaver Falls, with both working for Keystone Drilling. That's when she began to worry."

"Why?" both Fred and Sonja ask in unison.

"Everyone knew Carlton was trouble with a capital *T*. He got in trouble in school for stealing things. My mom used to say he managed to get out of jams because he was charming and clever. She called him 'a devil in a double-breasted suit.' Mom never trusted him, and Erik was powerless to get Carlton to behave sometimes."

I explain that Carlton as well as another man were named as suspects by the police in connection with my father's death.

"Sixty-two years later the case is still unsolved," I say. "The Steubenville police searched but never found either man. I was born six weeks after my father died."

"I know," Maja says. "Your Grandmother Eleanora told Mom that she tried to talk to Gracie on the phone a few times, but Viviana would answer and say Gracie was busy nursing you or she was sleeping. The police even called your grandfather in Glens Falls, but of course he knew nothing. I don't know if the police connected with Erik."

I tell Maja, Fred, and Sonja about the clues I found among Gracie's belongings. I also tell them Gracie received a letter from Carlton mailed from New York City two weeks after my dad's death.

"The genealogist I hired found Carlton's death certificate," I say. "It proves he lived in Sweden, but we don't know exactly why he ran away. Funny thing, though, my mother kept his letter to her hidden in her safe deposit box but never opened it. Why keep the letter but not open it?"

"Very strange," Fred says. "Maybe the heartache was just too much for her."

"Can you tell me anything else you can remember about my father?" I ask Maja.

"I recall that both your grandfather and my mother called Jefferson by the family nickname 'Junior.' Otherwise, I can't think of anything else."

Sonja suggests we return to Maja's house and use her laptop to try and find more clues.

"It can't hurt," she says. We all agree.

• • •

Sonja is sitting at Maja's kitchen table with her laptop in front of her while her mother stands behind the chair. "Does anyone want a cup of tea while Sonja is working?" Maja offers. We all nod.

"I've studied the Swedish language off and on over the years," Sonja says. "I can't speak it, but I can read most things. I'm going to see what I can find out about Carlton once he got to Stockholm in 1959. It will take me a bit, so Mom will fill you in on some information we've found on Vasterbottens County and the Bergstrom family during World War II. It's very interesting history."

Maja begins by explaining about the war on the Scandinavian Peninsula. "We all know Sweden declared itself neutral during the war, whereas Norway was occupied and Finland was aligned with the Germans but was not formally an Axis member. The German troops were stationed in northern Finland close to Russia. Denmark declared themselves neutral in 1939, but the Germans came in and occupied it in 1940.

"Technically, Sweden was then considered 'non-belligerent' or neutral but had some ties to Germany. That's because Vasterbottens County had lots of iron ore, which the Germans were anxious to buy. At the time, Sweden had 90% of Europe's iron ore extractions.

"My mother, Astrid, told me many of the Bergstrom men worked in the iron ore mines. The Germans purchased several mines in Sweden before the war broke out. Sweden needed the money. But Astrid was most proud that other Bergstroms were involved in the Resistance movement—both men and women."

"How so?" I asked, my curiosity peaked.

"For one, the Home Guard was created after the Germans started the war. The men were former soldiers who had guns, ammo, medications, uniforms, and supplies. Other family members and friends served as spies. Sweden allowed the Wehrmacht to use their railroads to transport German soldiers and weapons from Norway to Finland. All along the way, Sweden had civilians who spied on them. The passages were stopped in 1943. Sweden also helped train soldier-refugees from Denmark and Norway, and they sent 8,000 men to fight for Finland."

"Don't forget to tell Maureen about the other refugees," Fred says.

"Right—that was a big thing. Sweden took in 70,000 Norwegians and 70,000 Finnish children. They received 900 Norwegian Jews and 8,000 Danish Jews. Sweden did more than any other country to save Jews. It's terrible what the Nazis did."

"Eureka!" Sonja shouts. "I've got some information on Carlton. I found confirmation of a driver's license and a document stating he owned a cabin near Robertsfors. On both of those he used the name C. Erik Bergstrom. We already know he was killed in a fight in Kvarkenfisk in Umea. We now know where he is buried."

Sonja asks us to come and stand behind her so we can look at her computer screen.

"Here is his tombstone," she points. "He is buried in Robertsfors—Mellersta Kyrkogard—that is the Swedish word for 'churchyard.' He was 36 years old. So sad."

I stare for a minute at the image before me—a grave marker with the name Carlton Erik Bergstrom. This dead man is either my second cousin or my father. Which is it?

CHAPTER 28

I'm back in Steubenville, wrapping up Gracie's estate with the attorney. I decide to put the money from both the sale of Gracie's gold coin collection and the two bags of garnets I found to set up a nursing scholarship for local high school graduates. I will take the proceeds from the sale of Gracie's house in Mingo Junction and give half of it to Bridgette for the grandkids' college fund. The rest, including the old savings bonds, will go into my retirement accounts.

The Native American artifacts found by the police under the floorboards of Gino's cigar store will be given to a museum. The 400 shares of Carlton's garnet stock found behind a photo was bogus. No surprise there.

I get back in my car feeling satisfied that my legal obligations are completed. As I start the engine, my phone rings. I see by caller ID that it is the Steubenville police. What now?

"Hello, Mrs. Albrecht," Sergeant Gambino says kindly. "Can you stop by and see me? At your convenience, of course. I have some news and something to return to you."

"I'll be right over."

• • •

Gambino treats me like a friendly neighbor who is about to move to another city and is seeing me for the last time. "Well, Mrs. Albrecht, I think we can wrap up all our business today," he purrs.

"We can?" I say, amazed.

"Yes, we have checked out all the information you gave us plus some other information connected to your family. First, we have talked to my New York police contacts about the stolen garnets from the Barton Mines. They say their info is thin and the theft is not traceable, especially after all these years. It was probably an inside job—something that's a constant concern to them. They consider that case closed.

"We checked out the currency plate that was found in the wall of your grandmother's store to see if any money had been printed from it. We checked with the FBI, and they had nothing local on that matter, so that has been cleared," Gambino says.

I gulp at the mention of the FBI but feel somewhat relieved.

"As far as your father's death, we checked with Swedish immigration on Carlton Bergstrom and could find nothing illegal. We know he was killed in a fight in 1975, and we know he had a reputation as a fighter."

"Yes."

"We quizzed Charisse Duhamel, who was not even in Steubenville that night. She was with your mother out in Brimstone—that checks out. We also tried again to trace Duke

Maynard, our other suspect in your father's death. His brother, Sheriff Maynard, has been deceased for years, but his widow, Charlotte, lives in Cincinnati with her daughter. We talked to her, and Charlotte told us Duke, her brother-in-law, was a jealous man with a giant chip on his shoulder. Charlotte was not fond of Duke, and Sheriff Maynard wouldn't cross him. She said she suspects Duke wanted to go into the counterfeiting business with Jefferson but he wouldn't buy into it. Jefferson, apparently, did not want to cozy up with the Youngstown mob."

"Yikes," I blurt out.

"Duke also had plenty of debts with your grandfather and once tried to date Gracie. Your mother flat out turned him down. Charlotte added that she thought Carlton also wanted to date your mother. He was very fond of her. Duke died about 15 years ago in Wisconsin. He had never married, so Charlotte went up there to retrieve his possessions."

"I see."

"We checked out a few other leads, but they all came up dry. It's just been too long. But throughout this investigation we suspected your father's murderer was a man who was present at the fight club that night. It turns out that we were right. We're 99% certain we now know who killed Jefferson, and it wasn't his cousin."

Gambino pulls an old cloth handkerchief out of his desk drawer. The cloth has a monogramed *J* on it.

"A couple days ago we received a small package from Charlotte Maynard. This cloth item was inside," he says, handing it across his desk. "We think it belonged to your father."

I unfold the handkerchief and grip it tight.

"Oftentimes the killer will take personal items from their prey, sort of like a souvenir," Gambino replies. "It's all sick and very strange. One man dies of poisoning and two men disappear from here forever. Unfortunately, that was the norm in the Ville for many years, as you know from growing up here."

"Thanks for your efforts, Sergeant," I say, stunned.

"Two more things, Mrs. Albrecht. It's no surprise to you that your grandfather Gino received stolen items and resold them. He dealt with half the men in town, either gambling or fencing."

"Yes, the red ponies my mother mentioned near her death," I sigh.

"That's clear. I'm sorry about your loss. For all I hear, your mom was a good woman."

Gambino reaches into his desk drawer and hands me a small cloth sack. "Here's a little something to remember us by," he grins.

I peek inside and see it's filled with the garnets the police have held as evidence of a possible crime connected to Grandpa Gino's cigar store.

"We had a gemologist look these over, and they are high quality. They're worth a pretty penny."

"Thank. The proceeds will go to a scholarship fund."

"One final item. We received something else from Charlotte Maynard. She said to give it to you. She found this little box in Duke's possessions after his death."

I open the lid, which reveals a pocket watch. I flip the cover and see an engraving with the words *To Junior, Love Dad, 1955*. Below is the Celtic symbol like the one on Jefferson Sr.'s grave—a trinity knot. It must have been his gift to Jefferson as he went into the army.

I feel a flash of heat spread from my head to my toes. I can't breathe for five seconds. I pull the watch and the handkerchief in closely so I don't drop them.

"With this, Mrs. Albrecht, we consider the case closed."

I turn to leave the room and see Tim Konig standing at the door. "I'll miss seeing you around here, Mrs. A," he says. "Just remember, you taught me all I know. If nothing else, you are tenacious. You should have been a detective."

• • •

I'm sitting in Beatty Park with a letter I received an hour ago in the mail. I'm trying to summon the courage to open the envelope. It's from the genetic genealogist. Soon I will know whether Jefferson or Carlton is my biological father.

A young woman about 20 years old plops down on a bench across from me. She sets an old-fashioned boom box down next to her. I haven't seen one of those for 25 years. It seems very odd for someone her age.

The woman has long dark hair that drapes over her slender shoulders. I see tattoos on both forearms and one around her left ankle. I watch as she prepares to hit the play button—she is not wearing headphones. I brace myself for what will blast from the speaker.

Instead, what I hear is Antonio Vivaldi's *The Four Seasons* playing at a respectable level. Vivaldi wrote *The Four Seasons* *(Le quattro stagioni)* as four distinct violin concertos. It all takes place in a country setting. It starts in spring *(La primavera)* when the birds are singing. Next is summer *(L'estate)*, with more birds chattering, an alert to an approaching storm. After that concerto is autumn *(L'autunno)*. In this season, country folks celebrate the harvest by drinking wine. The tempo drops as they sleep—then picks back up. Finally, in winter *(L'inverno)* the folks tread an icy path. They fear tripping and crashing. The winter winds are cold and blustery.

I study the young woman closely as she embraces the music. Her eyes are closed and she is swaying slightly. I see her fingers start to move. Slowly she gets more animated. The concertos are written to flow from Vivaldi's musical interpretation starting with spring, then moving to summer, autumn, and winter.

By the time the piece gets to autumn the young woman gets more animated with her moves, as if feeling each note. With eyes still shut and a broad smile on her face, she waves her arms in round sways. About 32 minutes into the entire piece, the autumn concerto ends. Suddenly the woman opens her eyes and hits the stop button.

"Vivaldi," I say to her.

"Yes, I'm studying violin at the Cincinnati Conservatory of Music. I also play the clarinet. I like to come here when I'm home and listen to music. This boom box was my mom's. She died of cancer last year and it makes me feel close to her."

"You stopped before you got to the winter concerto."

"I don't listen to that part—my mother died during winter."

"I'm so sorry for your loss. My mom died in winter too," I say. "Do you mind if I ask if you attended middle school here?"

"I'm from Mingo Junction. I went to Indian Creek Middle School."

"My daughter, Bridgette Fellows, is the band instructor there."

"Wow, I had her in school! Tell her Grace Von Camp says hello and that I'm loving the conservatory."

"I will," I say as she hops up and trots off.

I think about this encounter for a minute. Her name is Grace—what a coincidence. She reminds me of a younger Bridgette—full of the love for music and determined to somehow make it her career. Secretly, I wish her the best.

I decide I've hesitated for long enough and now it is time to open the letter. After a few opening remarks, the correspondent gets right to the point.

> "We have examined both samples and the results are inconclusive. The DNA from Person A is most likely the father, but the DNA from Person B also shares long segments of DNA on several chromosomes. Further testing would have to be done. Please let us know if you want to pursue it."

Person A is Carlton—the man who is most likely my father. So, Charisse was right. My mother shared a love for two men. Carlton was no doubt jealous of Jefferson, but he was not my father's killer. I feel comforted knowing that fact. Further DNA testing may reveal he is my real father. Do I really want to know the definitive answer? Maybe this deserves further investigation.

My thoughts turn to Gracie. The Gracie I knew was the perfect mother. She was a real straight arrow—no trace of the free spirit she must have been before the death of Jefferson. She never dated again. Why did she suppress that part of her life? Instead, she poured herself into taking care of me and taking care of her patients at work. She was good at both.

I replay Vivaldi in my head. How things change—summer, fall, winter, spring. The composer who was also a priest. He saw death as part of life. The four seasons and the circle of life.

On this journey I've pursued for the last year, I've lost relatives and found relatives. New ones have been born; others have died. Life in a river town has a way of taking bad things and washing them downstream. There is a certain cleansing.

Life also has a rhythm and a tempo. I like to think of the passages of my life in musical accompaniment.

Mozart's "Requiem," Queen's "Bohemian Rhapsody," Alan Jay Lerner's "I Loved You Once In Silence," Bob Marley's "Three Little Birds," Led Zeppelin's "Kashmir," Bach's "St. Matthew's Passion," Vivaldi's "The Four Seasons."

It's something Steubenville's native son knew all along—something that is buried in all river rats' DNA. It's in me too. *That's Amore.*

ABOUT THE AUTHOR

Janet Shailer is an award-winning journalist and author whose nonfiction book *Trouble On Scioto's Waters* was selected for inclusion in 2022's Ohioana Book Festival. Early in her career she worked as a broadcast engineer at two NBC-affliliated TV stations and later became a writer/videographer for cable TV documentaries. She is the author of three children's books, three nonfiction history books, and one novella set in Appalachia. Shailer has also written for national and regional magazines and was editor of the *Southwest Messenger* newspaper. She graduated from Bowling Green State University in 1971 with a BA in Radio/TV/Film and a minor in Journalism. Her latest novel, *Murder in an Ohio River Town,* is based on Steubenville's history as a notorious gambling town. It is also the hometown of singer Dean Martin.

Made in the USA
Middletown, DE
20 September 2024

60721744R00142